SPENCER'S PROMISE

BROTHERHOOD PROTECTORS WORLD

TEAM RAPTOR
BOOK FOUR

DEANNA L. ROWLEY

Twisted Page Press LLC

I'd like to thank my editor, Ann Attwood, for the beautiful job she does on my books.

BROTHERHOOD PROTECTORS

ORIGINAL SERIES BY ELLE JAMES

Defending Evangeline - Delilah Devlin
Defending Casey - Reina Torres
Defending Sparrow - Jen Talty
Defending Avery - Regan Black

Brotherhood Protectors Yellowstone World
Team Wolf
Guarding Harper - Desiree Holt
Guarding Hannah - Delilah Devlin
Guarding Eris - Reina Torres
Guarding Payton - Jen Talty
Guarding Leah - Regan Black

SPENCER'S PROMISE

BROTHERHOOD PROTECTORS WORLD

TEAM RAPTOR
BOOK ONE

DEANNA L. ROWLEY

CHAPTER 1

FOOL'S GOLD, CO
  April

SPENCER BARNES LOOKED at the three empty chairs at the conference table and quickly became lost in the past. Staring at the three open seats brought back painful memories of the men he and his friends had lost on their last mission where they had done everything in their power to do the job assigned to them, but then they had been railroaded at the end by a man they never trusted and had lost their careers in the military because of this man. Thank goodness he was sitting in a jail cell, otherwise, Spencer didn't know what he would do. He was so bitter toward Walter Mathias that his body shook in anger when he thought about him. He hated bullies, and that was what Mathias had been.

"Ugg," Spencer snarled as he quickly stood, causing his chair to tip over as he leaned over the table, removed several items from his pocket, then slammed his fist down on the wood quickly three times. This caused the other four group members sitting at the table to jump up and stare at him like he had lost his mind.

"What the hell?" Simon Britton demanded as he looked at Spencer in shock. He quickly looked at what Spencer had done and saw the expressions of surprise on the other's faces. When Spencer turned on his heel to leave, Simon, Logan, and Nash quickly stopped him.

Nash Melendez stood before him and held his hands out, not touching Spencer, but he would if he had to.

"Whoa there, buddy." He looked at the other two men who stood on either side of Spencer, and after he received a nod from them, he looked directly at Spencer. "I understand you're upset, but you should calm down before doing something stupid."

"I hate bullies," Spencer ground out, and that was when Nash knew Spencer had been thinking about what had happened to the five of them over a year ago when they got back from a mission and lost their careers because someone, they thought had their backs, had lied through his teeth about them. Because of Wally's lies, the five men standing in the conference room had received an other-than-honorable discharge from their branch of the service. "What did you do to the table?" Nash asked Spencer calmly and saw the vein in his neck wasn't pulsing as hard as it had been when Nash had stopped Spencer from storming away.

"That's right, deep breaths, in through your nose, hold it, out through your mouth. Nash smirked when Spencer glared at him, but seeing Spencer follow his direction made him happy.

When he felt calm enough not to want to rip anyone's head off, Spencer stepped back from his friends and sighed heavily. He looked at the table and walked over to run his hand over what he had embedded into the wood.

"I should have been able to do this at their funeral if that Fuckwad, Mathias, hadn't lied through his teeth and got us kicked out of our careers. Harry, Joe, and Miquel were Seal Team 6, just like I was. To honor them, we keep these chairs empty, but I slammed a Trident into the table. If I had been allowed at their funerals, t would have put it in their casket." He looked at the others and saw understanding in their eyes.

"There is one good thing about all this shit that went down," Logan said as he leaned his hips against the table to study the rest of them.

"What's that?" Spencer snorted his response.

"The Fuckwad is in jail and can't roam around free. We may have been other-than-honorably discharged from our branch of service, but we're free to come and go as we please. I don't know about the rest of you, but when Hank came looking for us and offered us the opportunity to live and work here in Fool's Gold, I jumped on the opportunity to get the hell out of Virginia."

"Yeah," Spencer sighed as he looked at the others. "Sorry about going off like that. This isn't an excuse, but sometimes I think back to what that asshole did to us, and I see red. I hate fucking bullies, and that's what Wally Mathias is, a gigantic bully."

"Agreed," the others said, then paused as a phone went off. They all looked at their phones, and Spencer grinned. "It's me."

"Why the grin?" Darius asked with a frown.

"I have a lunch date." He put his phone away, then started toward the door.

"What's her name," Simon demanded.

"Seth."

"Excuse me?" The others looked at him in shock.

Spencer laughed for the first time in a long time at the expressions his friends wore. He decided to come clean and not mess with them, but he mentally held the right to do that later if warranted. "Seth Falco, remember, he and his brothers are with the local fire department. I ran into him a couple of days ago, and he said we should get lunch sometime when he was off duty. I don't know about you, but when I was with the teams, and he was in his unit, he was a Marine. We either worked together or passed on our missions. It'll be good to hook up with him and his woman."

"His woman?" Logan frowned at him.

"Honestly, I forgot her name, or I don't know if Seth ever told me. Anyway, I saw a ring on her finger, and I don't know if it's just an engagement or wedding ring. I'm going to lunch with them to catch up."

"Ah, have fun," the others said as they cleaned up their papers from their earlier meeting and finished their day.

"You're late," came a voice from behind Noreen, and she jumped because it was so close. She braced herself to face the wrath she heard in her co-worker's voice and shook her head as she turned toward the other woman.

"No, I'm not. I'm thirty minutes early."

"I told you to be here at nine."

"I know you did, but since you're not my boss, I came in at my regularly scheduled time."

"I need you to fill the condiments on the tables."

"Jennifer," came a stern voice from behind the two ladies. Noreen sighed in relief because Jennifer had backed her into a corner, and she didn't know how to escape it. They both turned to see their boss standing there with a foul look on her face. "*I* told *you* to fill the condiments. That's not Noreen's job." When the other woman didn't say or do anything except lift her head and look down her nose at their boss.

"That's what Noreen is for."

"No, as an employee of this restaurant, we all do our part. We help one another out. I need Noreen in the office. You've been here for over two hours, talking to the customers, and it's time you do the job I pay you for." Mattie turned on her heel and started to walk away but turned back and looked over her shoulder. "Noreen, please come to my office." Then she left.

"I hope she fires your lazy ass," Jennifer said to Noreen, and as she turned to leave the area, she made sure she bumped shoulders so hard with Noreen that she was pushed into the table by her side, causing the sharp corner to dig into her hip.

On the way to the office, the only thought Noreen had running through her head was that she hoped she wasn't about to be fired. She needed this job. It didn't pay as much as she liked, but with some intelligent budgeting, she could keep a roof over her and her daughter's heads and keep the lights on and food on the table. She did enjoy her job. It was just her co-worker that she couldn't stand. Being the last hired, Noreen wasn't about to make any waves with the boss and possibly lose her job.

She knocked on the door frame and smiled when Mattie turned with a grin on her face. "Come in, shut the door, and take a seat."

Noreen did those, then drew a deep breath and let it out slowly as she sat. She watched as Mattie rifled through some papers on her desk. Unable to hold back her fear, she blurted out her question.

"Are you firing me?"

"What?" Mattie looked genuinely shocked at her question. She studied Noreen, and after she laid the file she'd found on top of the papers on her desk, she settled back in her seat to study her employee.

"I'm going to be honest here, Noreen. I like you. You come to work, do your job to the best of your ability, and sometimes you even go above and beyond what's asked of you. I like that. Because of those work ethics. I will give you a raise."

Noreen sat there in stunned silence before she felt a gigantic grin cross her face, and she did a happy dance in her seat. "Thank you so much."

Mattie smiled with her as she pulled the folder she'd hunted down earlier closer to her and opened it. She brought out a piece of paper and handed it to Noreen. "What I just said isn't the only reason I'm giving you a raise. You're also getting one because it's your annual review."

"Holy moly, I've been here for a year already?"

"According to my paperwork, you have. Please, read that over, and if you agree with it, sign it. The new wage goes into effect today."

"Thank you," Noreen said as she quickly read it over and signed it. When she looked at Mattie to see if there was anything else, she frowned at the other woman. "What's wrong?"

"What I'm about to say stays between us."

"Okay," Noreen drew the word out because she saw Mattie's demeanor go from happy to disgruntled in less than a heartbeat.

"As I said, this stay between us. When I brought Jennifer in to give her the annual review earlier today, she wasn't happy with me. I've seen her act around you, and I fear she will take her anger out on you. The only example I could give was that she lashed out at you as soon as you arrived." Mattie held up her hand to ward off anything Noreen might have said. "I don't have proof, and if I ever have it, Jennifer will be out of here so fast all our heads will spin. I'm trying to say that I think Jennifer is stealing from the restaurant, but I don't have any proof. I know she's stealing time and called her out on it."

"What's that? Stealing time?"

"She's talking with the customers more than

doing her job and stealing time from me. I've also seen her leave the bussing of her tables for you to do. Please don't give her the satisfaction of doing her job for her. As I mentioned, she did not get a raise during her review. I shouldn't be telling you this, but I just wanted to give you a heads-up in case she tries to come after you."

"Thank you for being honest with me, Mattie. Can I tell you what I suspect she's been doing for the last three or four months? However, like you, I don't have any proof."

"What's that?" Mattie leaned forward and picked up a piece of paper to read.

"I think she's stealing my tips." Noreen dropped that and watched as the anger came over the other woman's face. "I can't prove it. I know I've seen customers put money on the table before leaving. I've been waiting on others or in the kitchen, but there's no money there when I go over to bus the table."

"Interesting," Mattie said and nodded. "I'll have to call my security guy to come in and see if he can put up some cameras. It's good to have extra security, not only for the customers but also for my employees. I want to know if you see her take anything as soon as possible."

"Okay," Noreen said, then knew she was dismissed, so she quickly left the office to go out and start her shift. She stopped at the workstation long enough to pick up a fresh order pad, made sure she had her pens, then went into the restaurant with a smile to start her day. As she grabbed her time card and punched in, she felt better knowing she was starting at a new pay rate. With a smile, she went to the dining room, tying her apron around her waist.

CHAPTER 2

SPENCER OPENED the door to the small diner downtown and had to pause to allow his eyes to adjust to the darker environment as he looked around to see if he could see Seth. Before his eyes were fully adjusted, he heard a voice from his side that made him cringe. With a curled look, he turned to the woman who had spoken.

"Excuse me?"

"I said, 'Aren't you a tall drink of water, and I'm parched.'"

"Then go get something to drink," Spencer said snidely and stepped to the side as the door behind him opened, and the man he was there to see walked in with a woman and another man.

"You're here," Seth said with a grin, then turned disapprovingly to the woman beside Spencer.

"Jennifer, we'd like a table for four, please."

No one said a word as she huffed, then flounced her body toward the front, where she grabbed menus, and without saying one word, she led them to a table toward the front of the restaurant. Spencer asked if they could have a table at the back. The woman Seth had called Jennifer glared at him, slapped the menus in his hands, and wrinkled her nose at him.

"Whatever," she said and walked away. Spencer looked at Seth with raised brows but shook his head and went further back into the restaurant. He wasn't trying to be difficult, but he wanted to do his catching up with his friend in a more private setting. Not that the middle of a diner was very personal, but it was better than where this Jennifer chick wanted to seat them. It didn't take long for them to settle. The only problem they had was that the men seemed to fight over who would be sitting facing the door, and the man who had come with Seth solved that problem quickly.

"Since I'm the local law, I get to sit facing the door." He grinned when the men acknowledged him, Seth held a seat for a woman, and Spencer waited until she was seated before they sat. Introductions were quickly made.

"Spencer Barnes, I'd like you to meet my wife, Kora. Kora, Spencer, the man I told you about. Though we didn't serve in the same military branch, our paths crossed several times during missions.

Next, we have Sheriff Jim Faulkner." Seth grinned at the other man as he continued. "Jim is joining us because we saw him on the street and invited him along. I hope you don't mind?" Seth turned to Spencer with a raised brow but continued before Spencer could answer. "Jim, Spencer is a former Navy SEAL, and he and four other gentlemen run The Centre outside of town."

Spencer held his hand out to the two people he didn't know, and they had to stop their conversation when the woman who had tried to hit on him when he'd first arrived came up to their table.

"What do you want?" she asked rudely, standing there with her pen poised over a pad of paper.

"Give us a few minutes, please," Kora said as she picked up one of the menus. "I will have a glass of ice water with lemon, though."

"I'll have a coffee," Spencer said, as did Seth and Jim. The woman wrinkled her nose at them, then turned on her heel and left, not saying a word.

"What's her problem?" Spencer asked as he looked around, and a sight caught his breath. On the other side of the restaurant was a woman that seemed to be running around to several tables filled with people, but to him, it looked like she floated as she walked. She had a messy bun on top of her head, and from a distance, Spencer saw it was a reddish blonde. Then he smirked when he saw her reach up and take one of the several pens sticking out of the bun.

"What are you staring at?" Kora asked.

"That woman over there." He pointed with his chin, and the others turned to look. With a smile, they turned back to him. Jim was the one to answer.

"That's Noreen Rafferty. She's new to town, well, not so new now. Been here for about two years. Don't know much about her, but I haven't had any encounters with her." Jim nodded and then looked between Spencer and Noreen. He caught Seth's look and reached up to cover his grin. When their waitress returned, they gave their orders and had to continue to wait for their drinks. As they waited, Jim looked directly at Spencer as he asked him a question.

"You work out at The Centre?"

"I do," Spencer said and studied the man intently. He didn't see anything in his expression that he wasn't happy with Spencer and his buddies' work, so he relaxed. "Was there something you wanted?"

"What do you do there?"

"I train all levels of Martial Arts and give self-defense classes."

"I want to sign up for your next class," Kora said and grinned at Seth. "Not that I need them, but you never know. After what happened with my stalker, fighting him off would have been better if I knew some defensive moves."

"I agree," Seth said, reaching over and taking her hand. He looked at Spencer and told him what had occurred when Kora had returned to work as a firefighter when he'd first moved to Fool's Gold. They sat back as their meals were delivered, and when Jennifer turned to leave, he asked if he could have the coffee he'd ordered earlier. She huffed and stormed away. As she walked away, he noted she had gone to the other side of the restaurant, and the table had just emptied. He watched as she moved the plates, and when she found some cash, she picked it up, put it in her back pocket, and walked away. Spencer exchanged looks with Jim, who shook his head.

"I don't know what the policy on tips is," Jim said.

"I do," Kora answered. "Why do you want to know?"

Spencer told her what he just saw, and she shook her head. "They don't split the tips here. You keep what is left for you. That said, technically, Jennifer stole money from Noreen by taking her tips. With my back to the room, I can't see what's going on. Mattie is having trouble with Jennifer, and I don't want to see anyone get fired, but if you see it again, see if you can't get her on video. I'd love to show it to Mattie, the owner."

"I'll see what I can come up with," Spencer said as he withdrew his phone and set it beside him. No one at the table said a word as Jennifer arrived with their drinks. She practically slammed them on the table, and once she left, they exchanged them, so they had the proper drink. Spencer turned to Jim. "Was there something you needed from The Centre?"

"Maybe," Jim said, and everyone waited until they took a bite of their meal, then chewed it. He shook his head and looked at the three at the table. "I don't know what to do."

"What's going on?" Spencer asked. He glanced over at Seth, who only shrugged and looked confused.

"I've had some complaints come into the office about some high school kids bullying others. I don't know if it's true or if it's someone trying to get back at someone. You know, trying to tattle on them to get them into trouble, or what it is."

"First," Spencer said, and it took everything he had to unclench his fisted hands. "I hate bullies. I might not look it, but I was bullied out of my career last year. Thank god the Fuckwad who bullied all of us, and in the interim, he got three of my buddies killed, but his ass is sitting in jail."

"Shit, were you court-martialed?" Seth asked.

"No, we were given an other-than-honorary discharge."

"Shit," Seth shook his head, then turned to Jim. "What do you think is going on?"

"I have no clue. Once I leave this meal, I'm heading to the high school to talk to the principal and try to get to the bottom of this." He looked at Spencer as they continued to eat. Spencer didn't see his look because he had turned his camera on and caught Jennifer taking cash off a table. He had seen

Noreen working since he arrived. He propped the camera up to see if he could catch her again.

"Spencer," Seth said, moving his head toward Jim.

"Sorry, what was that?"

"I'm heading over to the high school when I leave here. I was wondering what exactly you do in your self-defense class. What ages do you teach? What forms of Martial Arts?"

"All forms and all ages." Spencer grinned. "The youngest is a group of six- and seven-year-olds. I prefer them to be of school age, and of course, the parents have to sign a waiver."

"Let me ask you this, if I find out that there are some bullies in the school, would you be willing to come in and talk to them? I don't want to call them victims, but would you be willing to come in and talk to the people being bullied?"

Spencer thought for a minute, then nodded. "Sure, but instead of me talking with the victims, why don't we set something up with the administrators of the school that I come in and talk with the entire student body? Something like an assembly. I can talk about bullying and what it means, not only to the victim but also to the person doing the actual bullying. I can have some sort of release forms made out that would be approved by the principal, of course, about how the students can sign up for a class. We're not talking about this taking place overnight, are we?"

"No, probably not for a couple of weeks yet. It will all depend on what I learn at my meeting today."

"Okay, and if you need any references for my work, talk to Cog. I'm sure you know about the Brotherhood Protection Agency. They come to us over at The Centre to hone their skills. We have yoga, martial arts, and self-defense, this won't be for the students, but we also offer weapons training, as well as explosive training. We also offer survival training; you can also learn evasion, resistance, and escape."

"Wow, that's a lot of shit to learn."

"It is, but that and other duties were our specialties in the military. It doesn't mean we lose our skills just because we were bullied out of a job."

"True, true," Jim said as he nodded, then shook his head at something he saw. "I'll be right back," he said quickly, pushing his chair back and standing. He was gone before anyone could say anything. The three remaining at the table finished their meals, and as much as Spencer wanted another cup of coffee, he knew he wouldn't be getting one soon. He jerked to the side when the sexiest voice he had ever heard spoke at his shoulder.

"Would you like a refill?"

Spencer looked up into the greenest eyes he'd ever seen. They reminded him of a grassy meadow in springtime. "Please," he barely choked out, trying to unstick his tongue from the roof of his mouth. "Thanks," he said after she refilled his cup, then did the same for Seth. Before Spencer could say anything, she was gone.

"Are you okay?" Seth asked with a smirk.

"Fuck you," Spencer answered without any heat behind it.

"That's my job," Kora laughed at the two of them, and Spencer threw his head back and laughed along with her.

"And you can keep it." They continued talking for a few minutes, and Spencer looked up when he saw Jim approach their table with a woman in tow. He grabbed a chair and set it between his former seat and Spencer's. Once the woman had settled, Jim leaned his forearms on the table and introduced the others.

"I know you know Seth and Kora, but this is Spencer Barnes. He's one of the new guys that work out at The Centre. This is Mattie, and she owns this establishment." He didn't wait for his explanations. "I went to get Mattie because you saw Jennifer take cash off the tables Noreen waited on and saw it myself. Please, look at your phone to see if you caught it on video. If you did, please show it to Mattie." They all watched as Spencer did as Jim requested, and in no time, the evidence was shown. While they had been talking and eating, Jennifer had struck three more times, taking the cash from Noreen's table.

"Shit," Mattie said as she rubbed her forehead.

"Can you forward that to me?" She asked and gave him her phone number. Once it was done, she ensured she had received it, then looked at Jim. "I'm going to need your help."

"With?"

"I'm going to fire her. This is outright theft. I don't know if I can, but I'd like to see if I can't have Noreen press charges against her."

"Actually," Jim said as he sipped his coffee and shook his head sadly. "Because I witnessed it, and it's on film, I must arrest her. I'm going to need a clear policy from you on what the tip situation is."

"It's on my computer, but everyone keeps their tips. No one shares with anyone. Jennifer taking those tips from Noreen's tables is theft." She shook her head and looked out at the restaurant. What she saw made her cringe. Noreen ran around like her ass was on fire. All the tables in her section were full, and Jennifer sat on a stool at the front of the diner and played on her phone. The only table in her section was the one Mattie and the other four sat at.

"I know I can't tell you what to do, but can you guys do me a favor?"

"What's that?" Spencer asked.

"Don't leave Jennifer a tip. I know it's mean and possibly cruel, but I want to see if she does anything."

"Her service doesn't deserve a tip," Spencer said. "I tip on the service I receive. I never automatically leave a tip. If the service was good, then I'll leave one.

If not." He left the sentence hanging and shrugged. They saw some commotion on the other side of the room, and a table of six rose and left the area. Noreen was nowhere in sight, but Jennifer was off her stool in a hot second. Before Noreen reappeared from the back, Jennifer had scoped out the table and pocketed the cash she found before returning to her seat.

"Son of a bitch," Mattie said. "I want to call her back to the office now."

"Wait," Kora held up her hand to stop her. "I know I'm not with the law or anything, but Jim, don't you think Sparrow should be here?"

"Who's that?" Spencer asked.

"My female deputy," Jim said as he picked up his phone and sent a text. He sat back and nodded to them. "She's on her way, and thank you, Kora. I never thought to have Sparrow here. I can see where that would be in our favor. Jennifer is the type to call foul play if I was to arrest her." He turned to look at Mattie. "Can you wait until Sparrow gets here before doing anything? What time does Jennifer's shift end?"

"Not until three, but yes, I can wait. I'll be in my office." She quickly stood and headed back the way she'd come. She paused long enough to look back at Jim. "I'll get the policy and the copy of the one she signed when she was hired."

"Great, thank you." They watched the restaurant owner walk away, and Spencer shook his head.

"What?" Seth asked. "You looked concerned. It's not your fault."

"No, I'm always happy to help someone out. After what my buddies and I went through, I'm all for getting evidence. My only concern is will Jennifer go after Noreen, thinking she ratted her out?"

"There is that," Jim said as he sipped his coffee and watched the two waitresses do their jobs. Well, one waitress did her job, as well as Jennifer's, but he would withhold his comment until later, once he had the other women in the back room and arrested her.

CHAPTER 3

Noreen hurried into the waitress station and quickly made fresh pots of coffee. As they brewed, she filled the drink orders for her current table. As she waited for the coffee, she leaned her hands against the counter, hung her head, rolled it around several times to try to get the kinks out, and sighed heavily.

"Are you okay?" Came a voice to her side. After recognizing the voice, she only turned her head toward the woman standing there and wrinkled her nose.

Deanna, the cook at the diner, laughed. "Let me guess, Jennifer?"

"I swear to god she does nothing but sit on her ass all day," Noreen said as she straightened and began filling coffee cups for her order. Before she picked up her tray full of drinks, she heard something behind her and quickly looked back.

"What are you doing here?" She demanded, then shook her head as she exhaled loudly. "I'm sorry, that was rude of me. How may I help you?" She asked the gentleman standing there with a cup in his hand. She couldn't take her eyes off his face. She usually didn't like a man wearing a beard, but something about this man had her taking notice.

"Um, I'm sorry. I didn't mean to startle you, but I was wondering if I could get a refill on my coffee."

"Sure, I'll bring it right out."

"I can get it," he said, pointing to the fresh pot with the cup in his hand. Noreen watched as he did so, then couldn't take her eyes off his backside as he walked away.

"Who was that?" Deanna asked.

"No clue," Noreen started to say, then shook her head. "One of Jennifer's customers. I remember I had refilled their cups already. He must be important."

"Why do you say that? I've never seen him in here before."

"He was having lunch with one of the Falco brothers dating Kora. You know, the new bakery owner. Jim Faulkner was also at their table."

Before either of them said anything, Mattie was there. "Noreen, I hate to ask this of you, but could you hold down the fort for a few minutes? I need to have a word with Jennifer."

"Sure," Noreen didn't know what else to say to her boss. She secretly hoped Mattie could find a reason to fire the other woman. Not that she didn't want to see anyone lose their job, but waitressing was not for Jennifer. If sitting on her ass and playing on her phone was any indication. She watched as Mattie walked away, then turned to Deanna when the other woman grabbed her arm and told her to look.

"What the hell?" Noreen asked in shock when they saw Mattie leading the way. Behind her were Jennifer and the Sheriff, but behind him was the female cop, a woman by the name of Sparrow.

"Damn, to be a fly on the wall," Deanna laughed. "Let me know if I can help do anything."

"Right now, I must get these drinks out and take orders."

"Okay, I'll bus the tables as you do that. Where do you want your tips?"

"If there are any, then in my jar. It seems like I suck at being a waitress today because I haven't received one tip all day."

"Or," Deanna said with raised brows. "Jennifer took them before you could get to them."

"Do you think so? Because I could have sworn I saw the customers leave money on the table, but I had to return here. When I got out there to bus the tables, there wasn't anything." When Deanna did nothing but shrug, Noreen did the same as she picked up the tray of drinks and headed back out into the restaurant. For the first time in a long time, she sought out the man who had come back for a cup of coffee, and she liked what she saw. After she delivered the drinks and took orders, she returned to the kitchen.

"Nothing," Deanna said, and Noreen sighed heavily. She let it go, returned to the drinks, picked up the coffee pot, and returned to the restaurant. She went to her customers first, then over to Jennifer's table.

"WHAT DO YOU WANT?" Jennifer asked snidely as she was led back to Mattie's office. She stood before the desk with her arms crossed, her head lifted high, and she looked down her nose at her boss. "I have work to do. I don't have time to sit on my ass all day?"

"First," Mattie said coldly. "Drop the attitude. I've seen you, Jennifer, that's all you do all day is sit on your ass. I don't pay you to be on your phone during your shift." She picked up a piece of paper and handed it to her employee. "Is that your signature?"

Jennifer scowled as she took the paper and looked down.

"Yeah, what about it?"

"That is the paper you signed when I hired you that states your phone is not allowed in the dining area. It is to be kept out of sight of the customers. It also states that it has to be kept in your locker or your purse at the waitress station. It does not say you will be on it whenever you please. I've had several customer complaints that they can't get any refills on their drinks because they can't get your attention. I've had several customers go and get their drinks or flag down one of the other waitresses."

Mattie had to grit her teeth when Jennifer only shrugged and tossed the paper down. "Not my fault they're gluttons."

It took everything Mattie had not to jump to her feet and slap the woman across the face. She drew a deep breath and let it out slowly, trying to calm herself. When the restaurant owner, looked directly at Jennifer and said clearly, "You're fired for theft." "Before we go any further, I need to tell you that I'm within my legal right as the restaurant owner to tape this conversation."

"I didn't steal anything." Jennifer shrugged like it wasn't any big deal.

"One, you stole time from me. Several others and I observed you on your phone in the dining room. That's stealing time. I also have it on tape and by several eyewitnesses that you've gone over to Noreen's tables as soon as the customers leave and taken the money left there. That paper I just showed you with your signature also states that you earn your own tips. You do not share them with anyone else. It also means that you don't steal from others."

"If she's too lazy to take the money left for her,

then it sucks to be her," Jennifer shrugged again. This time, Sparrow came forward.

"Miss, I need you to empty all your pockets."

"Why? What the fuck are you?"

"I'm Deputy Sheriff, Sparrow. You are being arrested for stealing money from the tables you did not work at. I've seen the video, and I need you to empty all your pockets for my safety. Please remove your apron as well."

"I don't have to do as you say," Jennifer continued to be belligerent and started to walk away.

Sparrow reached up and took her bicep to restrain her. "Since I'm the police, and you are having charges pressed against you, you do have to listen to me. Now, for both of our safety, please empty your pockets." It seemed like Sparrow and Jennifer were at a standstill until the sheriff stepped forward, showed her the video Spencer had taken, and forwarded it to her phone.

"This is why you are being arrested," he said, watching as shock came over Jennifer's face.

"I'll kill that fucking bitch," Jennifer said as she whipped off her apron and held up her hands.

"Don't forget to empty all your pockets, especially the back right one," Jim said and nodded when Mattie held out a large plastic bag for the items to go into. They all watched as the items were emptied, and when they saw the stacks of bills removed from the pocket Jim indicated, no one said a word, but their brows lifted. When Jennifer said they were empty, Sparrow patted her down and nodded.

"I won't embarrass you by putting the cuffs on you as we walk out of here, but once we get outside to the squad car, I need to cuff you before I put you in. Can I trust you to walk directly from here to the front door without causing any scenes?"

Jennifer only shrugged, and as Sparrow led Jennifer away, Jim stayed back. He watched as Mattie counted the money. When she was done, she looked at Jim. "When can Noreen get this back?"

"When we leave here, I'll swing by the DA's office before I head out to the school. I'll see what he wants us to do. I know she will be booked, and it'll be up to the judge and DA to take it from here. How much was there?" He lifted his chin to indicate the money in the stacks. Luckily Mattie put them back the way they had been removed from her pocket.

"Noreen came in around six this morning, and it's almost two in the afternoon. Normally, she would have been gone by one, but I asked her to stay for a double shift. I don't know what's in the air or because it's spring, but we've been busy since we opened this morning, and we even had two tour buses come in."

"Okay, but that doesn't tell me how much money came from the pocket Jennifer put Noreen's tips in. I'm only asking because it matters how I present this to the DA."

Mattie drew in a deep breath and let it out slowly. "Eleven hundred dollars."

"Holy shit, then this just went bigger."

"How?"

"Anything over a grand is a felony charge of grand theft." He paused and looked at Mattie with wide eyes. "What in the world?"

"Sounds like Jennifer," Mattie said as they both rushed to the door and made it to the restaurant in time to see Sparrow wrestle Jennifer to the ground and slap the cuffs on her, reading her rights to her for the second time.

Jim rushed forward and demanded, "What's going on?"

"She tried to attack Noreen," Spencer said, wincing when he looked down and shook his head. "Over twenty years in the military, I was never seriously injured. Come home to a peaceful little town to settle down and get stabbed."

"What are you talking about?" Seth looked at his friend, then stared with wide eyes. "Holy fuck, how the hell did that happen?" He pointed to the steak knife sticking out of his upper chest, at his shoulder.

"She threw it at Noreen when she came at her yelling and screaming that she was going to kill her."

"Did you get it on your phone?" Jim demanded.

"I did," he let Seth hand the phone over to the sheriff, and when he went to pull the knife out, a small hand covered his, and the shock of the slight impact went right to his crotch. He looked down into the greenest eyes he had ever seen.

"Don't."

"Don't what?"

"Don't pull it out. You don't know if it hit something major. Let the doctors over at the hospital pull it out. Then they can stitch you up. Before it gets crazy in here, I want to say thank you for putting me behind you. As you can see, the level of that knife in your chest is level with my face. If it hadn't been for you, I don't know what would have happened."

"Glad I was here," Spencer said, gently raising his good arm to run his forefinger down her cheek. Spencer didn't know who did it, but he was suddenly shoved into a chair, and two people started working on him. Before they could say anything else, they heard the sirens of approaching vehicles. As he was loaded up on the stretcher, he looked at Seth.

"Make sure Noreen is okay." Then he was wheeled away, his last look at her was Kora standing beside her, and Seth lifted her chin to check her out. He knew she would be in good hands. Before being loaded into the ambulance, he called out to the sheriff.

"What's up?"

"I'll testify in court against that witch, and depending on what the doctor says, I may even press assault charges."

"Don't worry. It's on camera; I'm going to the DA

now to tell him what happened. Between you and me, she's facing felony charges now."

"Why?"

"The money we both saw her put in her back right pocket held over a thousand dollars. It will take some sorting to see if it was hers or all that belonged to Noreen. I can testify that she cleaned off at least six tables while we had lunch."

"Do you think any of this will come back and bite Noreen in the ass?"

"I don't see why she didn't do anything. I want copies of what the doctor says and does. I'll add them to the charges against Jennifer for your injuries."

"I'd normally say not to worry about it, but I've about had my fill of bullies. I'll do whatever I can to take her down. I hate bullies." He laid his head back on the gurney and gritted his teeth as he was loaded into the back of the ambulance. His last sight before the doors closed was Noreen standing on the sidewalk watching him. She looked so lost and forlorn that he promised to seek her out and tell her he was fine.

CHAPTER 4

"WHAT THE HELL?" Darius demanded the next day when Spencer entered The Centre with his left arm in a sling. "What the hell happened to you?"

"Long story," Spencer said as he used his right hand to grab his favorite mug and fill it from the freshly brewed pot. He took a bracing sip of the hot brew, sighed in contentment, and looked at Darius with a scowl. "The others in?"

"Yeah, they're in the locker room. Want me to call them out?"

"Please, I don't know if we will have a problem."

"Be right back," Darius left, and Spencer shook his head at the sling. The doctor said it was lucky he hadn't pulled the knife out of his arm because it had nicked an artery. He would have had significant blood loss if he had removed it without being near medical personnel. As it now stood, Spencer had received a total of twenty-seven stitches, both inside and out. He had to wear the damn sling for at least two weeks until the stitches were removed. On the ride to the clinic, Spencer had decided not to press charges against Jennifer, he would let the sheriff handle it, but since learning he would be out of commission, he had stopped by to talk to Jim on his way into work that morning. He had officially filed assault charges against the woman. He looked up as the others joined him and waited until they expressed shock at seeing him with his arm in a sling.

"What the fuck?" They all demanded at the same time.

Spencer held up his good hand to ward them off, and with his coffee cup, he leaned his hips against the counter. "Before I tell you what happened, I need some clarification."

"About?" Darius asked.

"Why did Patterson hire us?"

"Because he wanted someone to run The Centre with our capabilities. We were his second choice, but we're doing things right around here."

"Me too," the others said.

"Why?" Nash asked.

"So, we're not employed directly by the Brotherhood Protection Agency? We don't work for them?"

"Hank signs our paychecks, but we don't have to have assignments where we have to go protect people," Logan said. "However, we do have access to the branch of Brotherhood that is right here in Fool's Gold if we need them. Why?"

"Yesterday, you know I met Seth and his wife, Kora, for lunch, right?"

"Yes, did he do that to you?"

"No, I'm getting to it. When I arrived at Mattie's Diner down on Main Street, Seth arrived only a few minutes later. He had Kora with him, along with Jim Faulkner."

"The sheriff?"

"Yes, it turns out that he came along because he wanted to know exactly what we did here at The Centre. We talked about how he had to investigate but wanted to know if I could help him."

"With?"

"There has been a rash of bullying happening out at the school. The principal is concerned enough to call the sheriff in. He, in turn, wants to know what we can do to help these students. I offered to give self-defense classes to them, and I hate this word, but the victims of the bullying."

"What do you need us to do?" Logan asked.

Spencer fiddled with his phone, and when he had it where he wanted it, he looked at his buddies. "As I said, I arrived only a few seconds before the others. When I walked in, a woman said some shit like wasn't I a tall drink of water, and she was dying of thirst." Spencer scowled as the others snickered or outright laughed at him. He ignored them as he continued. "I told her then she better go get something to drink. She led us to our table, and we barely saw her afterward. When she did come to the table, she was rude, surly, and downright nasty, especially toward me. Anyway, I saw something out of the corner of my eye and began filming it. I later discovered I wasn't the only one to see it. Jim saw it too."

"What did you see?"

"When customers left from the other side of the room, our waitress jumped to her feet and went over to remove the cash they left behind."

"Holy shit, she was stealing someone else's tips?"

"Yes. Jim saw it several times, and we went to get the owner. She came out, we showed her what was on my phone, and well, let's say this Jennifer person wasn't happy when a female cop was leading her out." Spencer shook his head as he remembered what had happened next. "The other waitress was at our table refilling our drinks. As Jennifer came out, she screamed, broke away from Sparrow, and somehow got hold of a knife. All of a sudden, she was screaming that Noreen was a fucking bitch, as well as a liar, and she threw the knife. I immediately jumped to my feet, pushed Noreen behind me, and this is where the knife landed." He reached up and laid his hand over the thick bandage on his shoulder. He looked at the men as he said, "This was level with Noreen's face." Before anyone could say anything, he pressed a button on his phone. The others leaned in to watch as the money was stolen and the entire knife incident.

"Holy hell," they looked at him in shock. "What type of damage?" Nash asked. "Because you would have been the type to rip it out and not bother with the hospital."

"I am, but Noreen asked me not to. It was hard to resist," he smirked at them, and they shook their heads at him. "Anyway, the doctor told me it was a good thing I didn't pull it out because it nicked an artery, and I would have bled out and not known it. Internally and externally, I received twenty-seven stitches. At least I must wear this damn thing until the stitches come out."

"On the way in this morning, I swung by the Sheriff's office and filed an official report. I dropped off a copy of the medical report, as Jim asked. He wasn't in, but I hope to hear from him later today. If he does stop in, it's not because I'm in trouble. It's because of this."

"I can understand that, but why were you asking about Hank and The Brotherhood?"

"Because I want to run a deep background check on the worthless waitress. Something about her has my gut screaming that she's not done with Noreen yet."

"Why?" Logan asked.

Spencer looked at the men he'd been through hell and back with several times. He knew he could tell them almost anything. The ones that were right with him when they all received their other-than-honorary discharge from the service.

"I like here, okay. Not the bitch that did this, but Noreen, the other waitress. She's cute and has the greenest eyes I've ever seen."

"Ah," the others smirked and nodded several times.

"Okay, why don't you go to your office and give Jake Cogburn a call? Tell him what you told us, and ask if he can start looking into this Jennifer character. What's her last name?"

"Lockwood."

"Do you have any classes today?"

"No, it's a paperwork day for me. However, I'm thinking of setting up some permission slips for the students if it turns out anyone is being bullied at school. You know, pass them out and see if they want to come in and learn self-defense."

"Sounds good," they said, and they broke up then. Spencer refilled his cup and headed toward his office. Ten minutes after sitting down, he had Jake Cogburn on the phone.

"What's up?"

"Did you hear what happened to the diner yesterday?"

"I did. Sparrow told Stone, who told me when he came into work this morning. How are you doing?"

"Twenty-seven stitches in and out. She nicked an artery."

"Ouch. What can I do for you?"

"I want to hire you to do a deep background check on her. Don't ask me why, but my gut is screaming that she's not done with Noreen yet."

"Rafferty?"

"Come again?"

"Noreen Rafferty, small, petite, cute, reddish-blonde hair, green eyes."

"That's her. Don't get your panties in a twist, Big Guy. I'm happily married to my wife. I just wanted to clarify whom we're talking about. Noreen is a terrific woman. I don't know her story, but she and her daughter arrived in town about three years ago. Before you ask, I have never seen her with a man. She's good people."

"Thanks, and this Jennifer Lockwood, the wait-ress stealing from Noreen and throwing the knife at her. I happened to shove her behind me and took the hit."

"I've heard talk."

"Can you share?"

"It's not good. She's not known for her charm to begin with. Talk is that she hooks up with losers, and she kicks them out when they start kicking her around. The talk I've also heard is that she strikes out at others after a breakup. If I had to sum her up in a word, I'd say she's bitter. I hear where you're coming from and will do what I can. Are you pressing charges against her?"

"I am, I did so formally this morning, and on Jim's directive, I dropped off a copy of my medical records."

"Good for you. Give me a few days to get back to you about this."

"Thanks, Jake. Let me know how much I owe you."

"Don't worry about it," Jake said, and before Spencer could say anything, the line went dead. He shook his head and hung up the phone.

Spencer knuckled down and got to work on what he had planned to do that day, and it didn't take long to get into the zone of it. Though he hated doing the work, he knew it needed to be done if they wanted to get paid.

Several hours later, he glanced up at the knock on his door and quickly jumped to his feet. Standing in his doorway was the waitress he'd saved from yesterday.

"Hi, come in," he stammered, rushing around his desk to approach her.

"Hi, before we go any further, I don't think we were formally introduced. My name is Noreen Rafferty."

"Hi, Spencer Barnes." They shook hands and tightened their grip on one another at the slight tingle on contact. "Come in, take a seat."

"I don't want to bother you."

"No bother," Spencer felt his palms sweating and quickly wiped one down the outside leg of his jeans. He settled her down and saw she already had a bottle of water sticking out of her bag, but he asked anyway. "Can I get you something to drink?"

"I'm good. I thought I'd come and check on you. I didn't realize you worked here."

"Yes, I'm in charge of the self-defense and martial arts portion of The Centre."

"Do you train the public? Or is this some secret military or law enforcement thing?"

"I do both. Both the military and law enforcement, also private contractions. Do you know of The Brotherhood Protection Agency?"

"Yes, I know RJ. She's married to a guy named Jake Cogburn."

Spencer nodded. "I know Jake. I got off the phone with him a few hours ago. Before we proceed, I want to put my cards on the table. I was the one who used my phone to videotape Jennifer stealing tips from your tables. The first time I saw it, Jim Faulker saw it too. He was the one to suggest that I might want to get it on film. Later, after we saw her do it five more times, he went to get Mattie."

"Was that why she was sitting at your table? I thought it was because you were with Jim, and I know they are friends."

"I don't know about that, and without getting into

details, let me just say that I hate bullies. I felt that if she was stealing from you while not doing her own work, that was bullying. I saw how hard you worked and how little she did."

"For what it's worth, thank you. I thought she had been stealing from me, but I couldn't prove it. When I tried to confront her." Noreen paused and let the sentence die as she shrugged. "Yeah, I don't do confrontation well."

"I don't think anyone does. How are you?"

"Shaken up, but I'm good. The important question is, how are you? I see you're in a sling."

"I am until the stitches come out in ten to fourteen days. I have to thank you for stopping me. The doctor said the knife nicked an artery, and I would have slowly bled out and not realized it. I have internal and external stitches."

"I am so sorry."

"You have nothing to be sorry for," Spencer said as he rose from his chair and went to the front of his desk. He took her hand in his and held it gently. "If I hadn't shoved you behind me, you could have been seriously injured. I'll take the hit if it means you're safe."

"Thank you." They stared into each other's eyes for what seemed like hours, but it was only a few moments before he dropped her hand. Instead of returning to his desk, he took the chair beside her.

"Tell me about yourself."

Noreen snickered, which ended with a snorted laugh. "Are you trying to pick me up?"

"Something like that," Spencer answered honestly, then grinned as he reached over and closed her mouth with two fingers.

"You're serious?"

"As a heart attack. Are you single?"

"I am, are you?"

"I am. Do you have any children?"

"Does it make a difference?"

"No, I'm curious."

"I have a daughter. She's fourteen."

"That must be a tough age."

Noreen sighed as she settled back in her chair. "It is, and it isn't. Chloe is a great kid. Funny, smart, not what you'd call a typical teenager, but...." She paused and sipped water from the bottle she pulled from her bag.

"But?" Spencer asked gently.

"I think she's being harassed at school, but I can't prove it."

"Are there any signs?"

"When I ask about her friends, she says she's no longer friends. When I press the issue, she turns into the typical sullen teenager and won't answer. She either changes the subject or leaves the room. As much as I want to push, I know it might push her in the wrong direction if I do. I don't know what to do?"

"This might be out of line, but have you seen any bruises on her?"

"Why do you ask that?"

"Sometimes, when people bully others, the bully will be verbal, but it could turn into physical attacks. Take Jennifer, for example. She came out of the office yelling at you but grabbed and threw that knife. I was wondering if Chloe had any bruises on her arms." Spencer shrugged and watched, and Noreen looked off into the distance.

"Yeah," she sighed heavily as she admitted it. "When pressed, Chloe said she ran into a locker. I didn't buy it because one of her tells are when she refuses to look at me if she's lying. She wasn't looking at me when she told me she ran into a locker."

"I'm not pushing myself onto you, but do you think what we do here at The Centre might help her?"

"What exactly do you do?"

"I teach different forms of Martial Arts. Karate, Tai Quan Do, Tai Chi, stuff like that. I also run a self-defense class with some ladies in the community. I have a new one starting up next week."

"I can't afford something like that."

"You're lucky we charge on a scale." They didn't, but he wasn't going to tell her that. He would figure out what she could pay, then pay the balance. "Let me get you some paperwork." He rose and went around his desk to gather the information he wanted to give her. Once she took it, he took her hand in hers, and after exhaling heavily, he said,

"I don't know if I'm supposed to say anything or not, I'm probably not, but Jim and I talked yesterday. He had to go to the school because the principal had contacted him about serious bullying. I don't know if this affects your daughter, but he's gathering the information, then if he feels it's warranted, he will work with the school to call an assembly. He asked me to give a talk to the student body about bullying."

"Crap, so Chloe might be one of the victims."

"She might be. I won't pressure you, read over what I gave you, and here," he said as he leaned over and wrote on the back of a business card. "That's my cell phone number. The numbers on the front of the card are for here at The Centre. If you have any questions, you can contact me directly."

"Thank you, I will read this over." She held up the papers and stood. "I should let you get back to work."

"Okay, but I want to tell you something before you go."

"What's that?"

"I stopped by the sheriff's department this morning and turned in a copy of my medical records. I also filed official assault charges against Jennifer. I thought you should know if she tries to come after you. I don't know what's happening between you, but I want you to know what's happening."

"Thank you for the heads up. We'll have to sit down and talk one day when we have more time."

"How about dinner tomorrow night?" Spencer asked quickly. When she didn't say anything right away, he smiled at her. She must have liked it because he saw her sigh, then nodded.

"Okay, where and when?"

"You pick the place, say seven?"

"Seven, over at Gunny's bar. I'll meet you there."

"Deal," Spencer said as he grinned, then held out his hand to shake hers. They again tightened their grip on one another when they felt a tingle. Soon after that, Noreen left, and Spencer felt like he was walking on air as he followed her out and grabbed a cup of coffee on the way back to his office.

CHAPTER 5

NOREEN LOOKED up from the papers she was reading when her daughter walked into the kitchen. She didn't say a word, but studied her and subtly shook her head. Instead of saying anything, she pushed her chair back and held her arms out to her daughter. She didn't know if it would work, but she sighed in relief when her daughter threw herself into her arms. Noreen wrapped her arms around Chloe and held on. It was a long time before the girl lifted her head. When Noreen saw the tears, Chloe only shook her head at her mother, wiped her face on her sleeve, and sighed heavily before getting off her mother's lap and sitting at the table.

"Want to talk about it?"

"Not really, but I need to say something."

"Before you do," Noreen said, looking at her daughter. "Are you physically hurt?"

"Only a few bruises," Chloe said as she lifted the arm of her tee shirt, and Noreen saw the bruises on her biceps.

"What happened?"

"I don't know if you know this, but I've been having problems in school lately. It's nothing on my part. It's other people."

"Can you explain?"

"People are copying my tests. When I caught them doing it, I told the teacher. The next time we took a test, he moved my desk to a corner in front of the room. No one can see what I'm doing."

"I don't want to sound like a shrink, but how does this make you feel, and are you okay with it?"

"I am, Mom. I work hard for my grades. I don't need people who cheat to be in my life."

"Good for you. Is that why you've been so sullen lately?"

"Yes, and since I went to the teacher with my concerns, Brandi and her new posse are trying to terrorize me. It started with little verbal digs. You know, stuff about my hair or the color of my eyes. I ignored them as much as possible. We've had tests this week before spring break next week. Word must have gotten around about me going to Mr. Anderson about Brandi trying to copy off me because every teacher had a desk set up for me at the front of the room. I didn't question it, and when someone asked me why I thought I was so special, I told them that others were trying to cheat from me. I never mentioned any names, but they immediately knew who I was talking about."

"Can you say that she's being a bully against you?"

Chloe turned her head to the side with a frown, then nodded as she looked back at her mother. "Yes, Brandi is being a bully. We got into it today. After Algebra, she shoved me into the lockers and called me names. I didn't physically fight back but verbally fought her and her new friends."

"Can you give me an example?" Noreen asked as she rose from the table, turned on the tea kettle, got mugs down, and got their favorite tea bags out. As the water boiled, she looked at her daughter with a raised brow.

"In the hall, after Algebra, Brandi came right up to me, screaming for the entire student body to hear her, that I was a carrot top teacher's pet. She shoved me into the lockers. That's where I got these bruises. When you asked in the past about the bruises, it was because Brandi or one of her minions pushed me. I'm not in all my classes with Brandi, but she or one of her new friends is in my class. I verbally yelled back at her that I hated cheaters and that she and her friends were just that. Cheaters. That was why I took my tests at the front of the room. I didn't back down; we were even called into the principal's office. I didn't hold my tongue with the principal either. I told her exactly what Brandi and her so-called friends had been doing. That's when she told both of us that she was aware of the bullying and would call an assembly Friday afternoon." Chloe leaned back with a huff and shook her head. "She even said the sheriff and someone else would be there to talk with everyone. I know sticking up for myself won't win me any friends, but I can't allow her to treat me like she does. She's no better off than me but thinks she can treat everyone like trash because she's trying out for the cheerleading squad. I hope she doesn't make it." Chloe looked at her mother, and the grin on her face surprised her. "Mom?"

"Good for you," Noreen said with pride. "It makes me proud that I didn't raise a shrinking violet. Lord knows I need to stick up for myself." She then went on to tell her what had happened at work the day before, and afterward, once Noreen reassured her the man who stepped in front of her was okay, they shared a small laugh.

"Is he okay?"

"He is. His name is Spencer Barnes, and he gave me these when I went to see him." Noreen fixed their tea, and with the two mugs on the table, she showed her daughter the papers Spencer had given her about his self-defense courses.

"Can we afford to take them?" Chloe asked, which shocked Noreen.

"You'd want to do something like this?"

"If it would prevent this," Chloe said as she raised

the sleeves of both arms, and Noreen sucked in her breath at the uneven discoloration on both arms. They ranged from pale yellow to dark black. "But," Chloe said as she held up her hand. "I want to learn how to defend myself without getting into trouble at school. I don't want to be dispelled for fighting."

Noreen nodded. "I understand. Maybe I can mention that to him tomorrow night when I meet him at Gunny's."

"You have a date?" Chloe asked in awe. "Is he handsome?"

"He's not Mr. Universe, but he's easy on the eyes. He's tall, and I don't know how tall exactly, but well over six feet. Brown hair, brown eyes, and a full beard, but it's trimmed nicely."

"Where did you meet him?"

"At work yesterday. He saved my life."

"Mom, what the hell? Why didn't you tell me you were in danger?"

"First, don't swear. Second, it was handled nicely, but both Spencer and the police."

"Holy crap, the police were involved?"

"Yep. See, it started when I got to work. I was there at least thirty minutes before I was scheduled, but as soon as I walked in the back door, Jennifer started riding my ass." She grinned at her daughter as she picked up her teacup to take a sip. "I'm the adult, I can swear." They shared a laugh and settled back. "Anyway, Mattie wanted to see me right away. But not before telling Jennifer to back off and do the work she was told to do. Jennifer tried to tell me to do it, but Mattie had already told her to do it."

"Ah, gotcha. She didn't want to do it. Why were you called into the office?"

"I got a raise," Noreen grinned at her daughter's shocked expression. She held up her hand and shook her head. "You can't tell anyone because Mattie told me that Jennifer didn't get one. See, it was time for our annual reviews. I got more money, but Jennifer didn't. I know I harp on you to tell me what's bothering you, and I don't tell you what's bothering me. I could have sworn that Jennifer was stealing my tips from me, but I couldn't prove it. Long story short, this Spencer person saw her do it, and the sheriff were with him. He recorded my area of the diner during his lunch. I saw Mattie sitting with them at one point, but I was so busy, I didn't think about it."

"What happened?"

"At one point, all my tables were full. We had two tour buses come through. Anyway, Jennifer was manning the door, and she filled up my tables first. I could barely keep up, and when I went to bus the tables, there were no tips. I thought I saw the customers leave a tip, but I couldn't find it. It turned out I was right, and she was stealing my tip. Anyway, at one point, Mattie called Jennifer back to her office. I later found out she was fired. For not only stealing my tips but also for something Mattie called stealing time."

"Oh crap, that's bad."

"You know what it is?"

"Yes, it's doing what you want while on the clock and not what you were hired to do."

"Ah," Noreen said as she nodded her head in understanding. "Anyway, Sparrow was coming out of the back with Jennifer when suddenly, the witch screamed that I was a lying bitch, and she broke away from Sparrow. The next thing I know, I'm pushed behind this wall of muscle, and then Jennifer is face-planted into the carpet with Sparrow slapping the cuffs on her."

"Did you figure out what happened?"

"Yes, she grabbed a steak knife and threw it at me. It embedded itself into Spencer's shoulder here." She touched her shoulder to show her daughter where the knife had landed. "If he hadn't pushed me away, I could have been seriously injured because that area on his is level with my eyes."

"Holy shit."

"I'll allow that this time."

"What happened next?"

"Spencer went to pull the knife out, but I stopped him. The ambulance came and took him away. Jim took our statements and left. I finished my shift and came home. Today after my shift, I went to The Centre to see if I could talk with Spencer. It turned out he received twenty-seven stitches inside and out. That knife nicked an artery."

"He could have been in serious trouble if he'd pulled it out."

"Correct. But he told me he stopped by to talk to the sheriff this morning. He gave them a copy of his medical records and pressed formal charges of assault against her."

"Why was she arrested, to begin with?"

"Because Mattie pressed charges for her stealing time, and Spencer had it on video that she stole my tips. Mattie told me today that she stole over a thousand dollars yesterday."

"Holy crap, with that, we could both take these self-defense classes."

"We can, and though Jim stopped in and told me that money would eventually come back to me, I can't do anything until after the court case." She looked at her daughter and grinned widely.

"What aren't you telling me?"

"When they booked her and put her in jail, they found out the judge is gone on a fishing trip and won't be back until Wednesday next week." They shared a laugh, and together they gathered the papers and fixed dinner. As they ate, Noreen looked at her daughter closely.

"What?"

"Will you be okay by yourself tomorrow if I step out to meet with Spencer?"

"Will you be gone all night?"

"No, we're meeting at Gunny's at seven. I don't anticipate being gone longer than ten."

"Why so early?"

"Because I have the breakfast shift the next day."

"Ah," Chloe said as she nodded. "No, I don't have a problem with you meeting this Spencer character. I want to meet him."

"We'll see." Noreen left it at that as she helped her daughter clean up their dinner dishes.

CHAPTER 6

SPENCER WALKED into Gunny's bar at quarter to seven the next night and looked around. He smiled when he saw Noreen sitting at a table toward the back of the room. He started forward and paused when she looked up and stared directly at him. In his eyes, she was the most beautiful woman he had ever seen, and he couldn't wait to get to know her better.

"You're early," Spencer said as he approached the table. When she started to rise, he waved her back down. The first thing about Noreen that impressed Spencer was that she had left the seat facing the door for him. This allowed him to keep his back to the wall. The second thing was the fact that she was beautiful. Before he could say anything, a waitress showed up, and he gave his order, and again, it impressed the hell out of him that Noreen had waited to order a drink until he had arrived. When they were alone, she looked at him with a small smile.

"To be honest, I was nervous about meeting you. That's why I'm early." She looked at her watch and then back at him. "You're early, too."

"I am," he chuckled. "I, too, was nervous. I can't tell you how long it's been since I've been on a date."

"It's been a long time for me too. You're considering this a date?"

"I am, and I hope there will be many more after this." He held up his finger to stop her from talking and leaned back as their drinks arrived. When they were alone again, he looked at her with a smile. "How long has it been for you?"

"For?"

"Dating?"

"I haven't dated anyone since I told Chloe's father I was pregnant. That was fifteen years ago," Noreen sighed, then looked around the room behind her. Not seeing anyone close, she leaned in toward him.

"Can you talk about it?"

"It's not a light conversation for our first date."

"Yeah, but if we get the heavy stuff out of the way at the beginning, we can take it from there. Who knows, maybe neither of us wants to deal with the other's baggage. Better to lay all our cards on the table from the beginning. We can take it from there. We can even know if we'll get to a second date."

"How many second dates have you had in the past?"

"None," he grinned at her as he picked up his draft beer and took a quick sip. "Not that we got into the heavy stuff the first time. It was just that I never had any first dates."

"I find that hard to believe."

"Why?"

"You're a handsome man. Why wouldn't you be going out on dates?"

Spencer shrugged as he cocked his head to the side and studied her. "You think I'm handsome?"

"Are you fishing for compliments?"

"No," he chuckled. He settled in his chair and leaned toward her with his forearms on the table, cradling his beer. "To be perfectly honest, I lived for my job and didn't have time to date. If I did hook up with anyone, that's all it was. A hook-up. They knew going in it would be a one-and-done."

"Is that what you call a one-night stand?"

"It is. What about you?"

"I won't mention any names, but I started dating Chloe's father when I was fifteen. I guess you could say we were high school sweethearts. We even went to the same college and continued dating there." She paused long enough to take a sip of her wine and looked at him with concern. "Are you sure you want to hear this?"

"Yes."

"Okay, but it's not pretty." She drew in a deep breath, held it, wiped her hands on her thighs, then let the pent-up breath out in a rush. "When I realized I was pregnant, I went to him and told him about it."

"How did he react?" Spencer asked after several moments of silence.

"I thought he took it in stride. He didn't deny it, get mad, or tell me I was lying. I told him two days before we were to go home for spring break. See, after we left for college, his father was transferred, and the rest of his family moved to a different state. I don't know if this means anything, but his father was in the military." She studied him and saw understanding in his expression and breathed easier.

"Anyway, we were still together before we left for the break and had decided not to tell our parents until we could do it together."

"What happened?" Spencer asked when he saw the sadness come over her face.

"I knew I couldn't talk to him often over the break. He said his family wanted to show him the new area they had moved to. Anyway, I returned when we were supposed to, and it was a couple of days before I realized I hadn't seen him. Several mutual friends said he had transferred to a different college during the break. He never told me he did that, and the last time I saw him was the day we left for spring break."

"Holy shit," Spencer said in shock. "What happened next?"

"I waited until after graduating college and told my parents what had happened." She looked at him with a scowl. "Do you want me to nutshell it or drag it out?"

"Nutshell."

"They disowned me."

"Holy shit." He sipped his beer, trying to wrap his head around what had happened to her. "Okay, a little more detail."

Noreen smiled and nodded. "When I told them what happened after I told him, they did some investigating. My parents and his were best friends when they lived where we did. Dad contacted them and explained the situation. I don't know what all went down, but again, in a nutshell, he didn't want to be pinned down with a kid, so he had his parent's lawyers draw up papers that he renounced his involvement in the child's life."

"Does your daughter know this?"

"Yes, but I only told her last year."

"Does she have your last name?"

"She does."

"How did your parents disown you? How old were you at the time?"

"I was twenty when I found out I was pregnant and twenty-one when I had her. They told me that because I had sex outside of marriage, then I wasn't their daughter. I had disgraced them by getting pregnant. See, they thought they were the pillars of the community, but they were hypocrites. It was like a do as I say, not as I do type of situation. Outside the home, they were the best people to be around. Inside was a different story."

"Were they abusive to you?"

"Not so much abusive. I would say it was more like lazy."

"Can you explain?"

"Hoarders."

"Excuse me?"

"My parents were hoarders. But it wasn't as bad as you see on that TV show. There wasn't any garbage or anything like that, and the house didn't smell, but Mom would hoard clothes. We lived in a four-bedroom home with a finished basement. When I was ten, I moved to the basement. It had a bathroom, a small kitchenette, and a private entrance. We were going to rent it out at one point, but I took it over, and they took over the entire upstairs." She sipped her wine and rubbed her forehead before she looked at him again. "When I left for good, every bedroom upstairs had full closets, and Mom went out and bought more hanging racks and hangers. A department store was going out of business, and she got all the racks and tables from that store."

"Shit," Spencer said as he sipped his beer. "One question, were these clothes clean or dirty?"

"Clean. As I said, they weren't filthy. They just had so much shit. The weird thing about it was that she didn't spend a lot of money on the clothes."

"What do you mean?"

"She bought all her clothes at second-hand stores or garage sales. You know, a pair of jeans for a dollar, stuff like that. That was how I was raised. The only items you bought new were what touched your skin —you know, bras, panties, and socks. Everything else was second-hand. Mom had it down to a science where she could get good deals on some great name-brand clothes. The only downfall was that she never resold them or got rid of them in any way."

"Wow, that must have been rough." He sipped his beer again, then looked at her with a grin. "Do you ever wonder if they took over the basement after you left?"

Noreen had been sipping her wine and snorted a laugh, causing it to come out of her nose. She grabbed a napkin, and after she cleaned up the mess, she threw it at him, laughing. "I can see the arguments they would have had. They probably divided it like they did the rest of the house."

"What do you mean?"

"The bedrooms were on the second floor. Mom took over all of them, even the spare bathroom. That she filled with towels, sheets, and spare blankets. Anything to do with fabric, she hoarded it."

"What about your father? What did he hoard?"

"Promise not to laugh?"

"I promise," Spencer said, lifting his hand with three fingers, indicating the Boy Scout promise.

"Kitchen appliances." She held up her hand at his shock. "I kid you not. He was the same way Mom was. When I left for college, we had at least sixteen different bread makers, ten mixers, the hand-held type, and the same amount in the countertop versions. I lost count of how many air fryers, crock-pots, and everything else. Not one of those items was bought new at a regular store. He purchased them at thrift stores or garage sales."

"Did he use them?"

"Last I checked he did. But they were all over the house. The last time I was there, they had all the rooms full except for one. That was the living room, where they would occasionally entertain guests. That was what they called the 'neutral room.' All hoarding was off limits there."

"What about you? How did you grow up?"

Spencer shrugged and shook his head. "I guess you could say normal. I lived in a happy home with my parents and two siblings. I'm the middle child. I have two sisters. We lived in what you would call a small town USA. We had neighborhood block parties or picnics in the park. When I was old enough, I would hire myself out to shovel sidewalks and drive-ways in the winter and mow lawns in the summer. I guess you could say I grew up like the Cleavers."

"No offense, but you don't seem the type."

"Yeah, what I did after leaving home made me the way I am now."

"What did you do?"

"Joined the military."

"Ah," Noreen said, then studied him for several minutes. She didn't know why, but she reached out to lay her hand over one of his. "Do you want to talk about it?"

CHAPTER 7

"ARE you sure you want to know?"

"Hey, you said we should lay all our cards on the table. I told you about Chloe's father and my parents, and it's your turn."

"Okay, but you never told me why they kicked you out."

"I did. It was because I disgraced them. I left and moved halfway across the country. I'll save it for the third date to tell you where I'm from." She grinned at his snorted laugh. "Let's just say I left and got on with my life. My last contact with them was when I gave birth to Chloe. I asked if they wanted to know what I had, and they said no, and hung up on me. I haven't contacted them since."

"Wow, that's cold."

"It was. I'm not saying it was all sunshine and roses because it wasn't, but it was eye-opening. It made me grow up and become a parent. I vowed to be better than they were. I learned from my mistakes along the way, and now I control what I do with my life."

"Please don't think this next question is a dig because it's not, but why are you a waitress?"

"Because I like it. I meet new people, or my regulars, all the time. I see them for maybe an hour, then move on to the next group. I'm a people person, and I've found that waitressing has been my jam over the years. It's hard to explain, but I'm okay as long as I'm waiting on people and keeping busy. It helps when I interview for a job, and I tell them I'm a single mom, and they work around my schedule."

"Have you always been a waitress?"

"No, I used my degree and worked in offices until we moved here about four years ago. Now, you're dodging the question. Let's say that I find being a waitress more stimulating and challenging than working in an office. What happened to you in the military?"

Spencer finished his beer, then held up his glass, and neither of them said a word as a refill was brought for them both, along with a bottle of water for Noreen. She'd finish the second glass of wine, then switch to water, if not before.

"I joined the Navy right out of high school. I was in for about four years before I applied to become a SEAL.

It was hell, but I passed and received my Trident. That's the pin to prove you're a SEAL. Anyway, I served my country and did my duty. I loved what I did and did it for years. A few years after becoming a SEAL, I was invited to join a special task force for special projects. I can't give names, locations, or details, but I can tell you that the special task force I joined was JSOC. This stands for Joint Special Operations Command. It's where a group of the best people from all military branches gets together for one mission. I had been on several of them before and the other men I work with at The Centre." He paused and sipped his beer.

While looking at the table, he continued, "As I said, we had been on several missions before. The man in charge was a Fuckwad. Sorry if that offends you, but he was an ass. I can't say who he is or what he did, but he was the biggest asshole that walked the face of the earth." He looked up and saw understanding in her expression and continued. "It didn't take us long on our last mission to realize we had been lied to by the Fuckwad. It bit us in the ass when we returned."

"How?" Noreen blurted out. She reached out and covered his hands with one of hers. "I won't ask what happened because you probably can't tell me. Can you tell me how it bit you in the ass?"

"He lied to us and turned in false documents. Because of his lies, three great men and soldiers are dead, and the five of us were given an other-than-honorary discharge."

"What's that?"

"The twenty-three years I put into the service amounts to nothing. Because of the Fuckwad lies and deceit, we lost our pensions, military status, everything."

Noreen could see he was becoming upset and gently squeezed his hand. "Where is this Fuckwad now?" She sucked in her breath when he looked up at her, and she could only describe his expression as an evil grin.

"His ass is sitting in jail."

"Oh, wow. I know you can't tell me, but how did that happen?"

"During our trial, someone gathered information that helped us, not him. See, it turned out the Fuckwad wanted all of us dead. He hired some nasty people to take us out. He got three of us killed, and he's in jail now. He won't be seeing the light of day anytime soon. They stripped him of his credentials and importance the way he had ours stripped. The only difference is that we're free, and he isn't."

"Was there a chance of you going to jail?"

"No. Because of what happened, I've learned to document everything. That's why I used my phone to videotape Jennifer stealing your tips. I don't trust anyone with important information. If I can, I will get proof. I've learned my lesson after working with Fuckwad."

"I only have one question. Why did he want you dead?" Then we can move on.

Spencer sipped his beer, wiped his mouth, and grinned at her. "Because we're good at what we did."

"I don't understand."

Spencer leaned back in his chair and looked at her intently. "Remember, I said that the best of the best from several military branches joined that special task force?"

"Yes."

"Well, we had worked with the Fuckwad on a few missions before the last one. Every time, one of us would overrule what he wanted us to do. We even went so far as to go over his head. The higher-ups took our side, not his. I'm talking about his bosses."

"Wow, that must have gone over like a lead balloon."

"It did. Each time it happened, Fuckwad was pissed. At the end of one mission, he warned us not to fuck with him anymore and that we would regret not taking his orders." Spencer leaned forward and brought his head closer to hers. "See, he was pissed because we survived the missions he put us on, and we came out smelling like roses, where he didn't. I can't tell you how many times his superiors yelled at him. Before you ask, he was not military. Anyway, that last mission that bit us in the ass, it turned out that Fuckwad hired insurgents to kill us. He didn't give a damn about the mission we were on. He wanted us dead. He only succeeded in getting three of us. For his lies, deceit, and overall Fuckwadness, he's now sitting in jail with three murder charges over his head. At the same time, we had to start all over with no pensions. Hank Patterson from the Brotherhood Protection Agency came to us and hired us to run The Centre. That was how we were able to get back on our feet."

"Wow," Noreen said as she shook her head and picked up the water bottle to sip. She abandoned her untouched glass of wine.

"And you're okay now?"

"We're getting there. Since we're laying all our cards on the table, I can tell you right now that I abhor two types of people and will not associate with them in any manner. They are liars and bullies. That's what Fuckwad was. He lied and bullied us, as well as others, into our getting the other-than-honorary discharge."

Noreen studied him intently and nodded once. "I understand, and I feel the same way." She drew in a deep breath and let it out slowly. "Can I ask you a question?"

"You may."

"Has the sheriff been able to talk to the principal?"

"He has, and on Friday, there's an assembly that he invited me to attend. I'll talk to the entire student body about bullying and pass out flyers to see if I can't get some students to sign up for my self-defense classes. Was there any particular reason why you're asking?"

"Yes, I had a nice talk with Chloe yesterday. She finally admitted her former best friend is bullying her." Noreen ran her hands up and down her upper arms and shook her head. "She showed me the bruises on her arms where this friend has been pushing her into the lockers." She shook her head again and chuckled. "I know this isn't a laughing manner, and please don't think I'm laughing at them. I'm laughing at what my daughter said she did next."

"And that was?"

"She stuck up for herself. I am so proud of her. The way she said it was that she wasn't going to take any shit from anyone, and if she was called to the principal's office, then so be it, but she would tell her side of the story and take the consequences if there are any. So far, from what Chloe's told me, there hadn't been any for her. I don't know about the one bullying her."

"Do you know what started it?"

"A little, see Chloe and this other person have been best friends since we moved here before they started kindergarten. Chloe's smart. She's on the high honor roll every semester and takes her schoolwork seriously. One day, she realized her friend was copying her answers on a test, and after class, she told the teacher. But she took it one step further and went to the principal. This week, the kids are taking mid-term exams, and so far, in every class, Chloe has been set apart from the others at the front of the room."

"Good for her and for her teachers believing her. I feel something happened."

"It did. The friend took offense at not being able to copy off Chloe in Algebra. After that class, the friend shoved my daughter into the lockers, and she has bruises on her arms."

"You realize that's assault, right?" Spencer asked and saw shock come over Noreen's face. "It is, as soon as someone puts their hands on you, that's assault. Your daughter can press charges, or you can, because your daughter is under the age of eighteen. That's something you'll want to look into."

"Shit, I never thought of that." Noreen shook her head. "Anyway, a teacher saw what happened, and I don't know what the final results were, but I do know that Chloe didn't back down and told the principal exactly what happened. Chloe was dismissed, the friend had to stay back, and now there's an assembly happening on Friday."

"The one I'm going to be attending?"

"Yes. I told you all that because Chloe and I talked, and she wants to take the classes. Not necessarily the martial arts, but she wants to know how to defend herself so she's not being bruised and bloodied when she's being shoved around. Can you do something like that?"

"I can. I can teach her how to move so that she doesn't get hurt, and she's not placing her hands on the other person."

"We wouldn't want that."

"No, we wouldn't. I can even teach you the same moves."

"Why would I want to learn that?"

Spencer looked at her with a raised brow. "Call me paranoid, but think about it. If Jennifer is still in jail until the judge returns next week, will she let it go? She already thinks you're the one that blew her in for stealing your tips. She proved that when she threw that knife at you."

"Speaking of that, where's your sling?"

Spencer shrugged. "Didn't need it. Besides, it was a pain in the ass to wear."

Noreen snorted a laugh. "Big tough guy?"

"Something like that. But seriously, Noreen, you need to know how to defend yourself against a personal attack. You never know when someone will come at you." He studied her and shook his head at her when he saw her expression. "Don't. Don't blow this off. Think of how strong you said your daughter is. I'm sure she gets that from you. Don't disappoint her by not taking care of yourself." When he saw she still wasn't taking what he said seriously, he went in for the kill. "Who will take care of her if something happens to you?"

"That was a low blow, Spencer."

"I know, but your safety isn't a laughing matter. You need to take it seriously."

Noreen turned her head and looked down her nose at him. "I'm not saying I'll do it or won't, but do you have a payment plan?"

"We can work something out."

"Can I think about it?"

"Yes." Spencer leaned on his hip, withdrew his wallet, and pulled out a card. "Here's my card."

"I already have it at home."

"Keep this in your purse." He wrote on the back of it and handed it to her. "I don't want to be morbid, but if something happens to you, you'll have my card on you, and they can contact me. I'll be your contact person."

Noreen could tell from his expression that she was fighting a losing battle, so she took the card with a small thank you. They sat silently until she looked at him and asked, "So, what now?"

"What do you mean? What now?"

"Do we see each other again? We laid some heavy baggage on the table for our first date. I'm not putting any pressure on you, but from where I'm sitting, I would like to see you again."

Spencer felt like his face split in half with the grin that came over him. He reached across the table and took one of her hands in his. "I'd like that. From what I've learned about you tonight, I heard nothing that would drive me away." They sat like that for several minutes, holding hands and staring at one another, until Noreen gently squeezed his hand.

"I hate being a party pooper, but I must get home. I know it's early, but I have the breakfast shift tomorrow. That means I need to be at work by five."

"Wow, that's early. Do you always work the breakfast shift?"

"No, not always. I work either in the mornings or afternoons. I don't work the evening crowd." She saw he would ask why, so she answered before he could ask. "I like to be home at night with Chloe. She's at the age now where she can get herself up and off to school. That's why I work mornings sometimes now. I like to be home at night to either go to one of her after-school activities or make sure she had a hot meal and help her with homework."

"I understand," Spencer said. "When can I see you again before I walk you to your car?"

Noreen frowned as she did a mental check of what her schedule was like for the next few days. "How about Sunday afternoon? I have that day off and like to do my housework in the morning, but I'm free in the afternoon."

"Perfect. Will you include Chloe on this date?"

Noreen looked at him in shock. "Do you want me to?"

"Why not?" Spencer shrugged. "If we're getting to know each other, why not include her? She's going to want to know me, and vice versa."

"I'll talk to her about it."

"Sounds good." Spencer rose to his feet, then helped her from her chair. He also took her light jacket off the back of it and held it for her. With his hand on her back, he escorted her out of the bar and to the parking lot.

"This is me," Noreen said as she headed toward a small SUV. She looked at Spencer in shock when he grabbed her arm and pulled her back.

"Wait here," he said as he approached the vehicle. He walked around it, and she heard him swearing. Something about the way he held himself had her staying where she stood.

"What is it?" She asked as he came back around the vehicle and faced her.

"Someone slashed your tires."

"What?" She screeched, then turned at the roar of an engine, and the next thing she saw was Spencer as he flew through the air, and she landed in the dirt several feet away, with Spencer on top of her.

CHAPTER 8

"Are you okay?" Spencer demanded as he rolled off her, but he wouldn't allow her to get up until he checked her out. When he felt no broken bones, he helped her to his feet and looked up when several people came running from across the parking lot. They were shouting to see if they were okay.

"I called 911," someone in the crowd said, and they all lifted their heads as they heard sirens in the distance.

"What the hell is going on here?" Demanded a gruff voice, and Spencer turned to see Gunny standing at the crowd's edge.

"Barnes? Is that you?"

"Yeah, Gunny, it's me. It seems we've had an incident here in your parking lot." He wrapped his arm around Noreen and felt her shaking. He leaned down and whispered in her ear. "I've got you." She seemed to like that because he felt her burrow into his side and found he liked her there.

The others in the crowd told Gunny what they saw, and Spencer remained silent until the police arrived. He didn't know if he was relieved or worried when it was the sheriff who arrived.

"What's going on?" Jim Faulkner asked as he came up to them.

"Noreen and I were here on a date," Spencer began. The others in the crowd quieted down and listened to him. "When we came out to go home, I noticed her SUV looked off."

"Off, how?"

"Uneven," Spencer said as he pointed to it, and everyone turned to look. "I had her wait here while I walked around the vehicle. Both tires on the other side are sliced."

"Both?" Noreen asked in shock.

"Yeah," Spencer said as he held her tighter, then looked at Jim. "I just came back around the vehicle when I heard the roar of an engine. I didn't get a look at who or what it was. The lights were blinding. I only had enough time to dive on top of Noreen to get us both out of the way."

Jim nodded as Spencer talked, then he walked around the vehicle. When he came back around, he shook his head in Noreen's direction. "I'm sorry. Barnes is right, and you have to flat tires. I'll call a tow truck for you."

"Wait," Noreen said as she stopped him from pulling his phone out of his pocket. "I have two spare tires." When she saw both Jim and Spencer's shock, she shrugged. "When I bought the vehicle, the spare was mounted on the bottom of the truck. About two weeks ago, I decided to get it out from under there and put it in the back. I couldn't get it. I'm glad I did because I ended up having to take it to a garage and have them remove the tire. When the man at the garage put the spare in the back, he found a donut. I told him to leave it there."

"Spencer?" A man asked from the crowd, and everyone turned to see several men and women approach.

"Darius," Spencer said. "What brings you guys here?"

"Thought we'd stop in for a drink. What's going on?"

Before he answered, Spencer looked around and saw the sheriff taking statements from people in the crowd. Then, with his arm still wrapped around Noreen, he indicated with his chin for them to step off to the side. When they were away from people, he looked at his friends. "Noreen and I were here on our first date. I was walking her out to her vehicle when it looked odd. I checked it out. She has two slit tires on the other side."

"The side she wouldn't have noticed if she was alone."

"Correct. I don't think she wouldn't notice, but you never know. Anyway, I walked around the truck, and we heard a loud engine when I returned to her. Someone tried to run us over, and I grabbed her and hit the dirt. Other people in the lot saw it and called it in. Jim's only been here for a few minutes before you arrived."

"Do you have a spare?" Logan asked. At her confused look, he smiled at her. "Logan. I work with Spencer up at The Centre."

"Ah, okay. Yes, I have a full spare and a donut."

"Can we change them?" Someone else asked, and he looked at Noreen with a smile. "Simon."

"Okay. Why couldn't you change them?"

"Jim might want to see them."

"Couldn't we give him the tires after we take them off? I'm not trying to be a bother, but I'd like to get home." She wrapped her arms around her and ran her hands up and down her biceps like she was cold. Spencer hugged her to him and looked at the others.

"We'll take care of it," Simon said. "Why don't you let Spencer take you home?"

"What about my truck?"

"Give us your address, and we'll bring it to you," Logan said. "If it makes you feel better, Spencer can stay until you arrive. It shouldn't take us more than half an hour to do this."

"I can't ask that of you."

"You didn't ask," someone else said. "I'm Nash.

We're volunteering. Some of us will even stick around and talk with Jim."

Noreen was uncertain about doing what they suggested, but the matter was taken out of her hands when Jim returned to them. "I overheard what the boys said. I agree with them. Let Barnes take you home and have the guys change them for you. I won't need the tire until you take it to the garage and fix it. I'll call them in the morning with a heads up."

"I can't get to the garage until after my shift. I get out of work at two."

"That will be fine. Let me get the size you need, and I'll make sure the garage has two in stock." He walked away, and Noreen thought she heard the sound of a camera but didn't comment on it. She looked at the people around her and felt no fear or misgivings. Something about them made her feel safe.

"Okay," she sighed as she dug into her purse, withdrew a set of keys, then took the truck keys off the main ring. "These are the truck keys. I live out past the City Park. About three miles out." She gave them the physical address and thanked them before Spencer led her across the lot to his truck. No one said anything until the couple pulled out of the parking lot.

Darius turned to Jim with a scowl. "What do you think? Do you think she was the target, or was this aimed at our boy?"

"Honestly, right now, I have no clue." He held up his hand to stop them. "I'm not ruling anything out. I've got both their statements and the people in the crowd." He shook his head tiredly and pinched the bridge of his nose. "I have no clue what to make of this. I'll check into it when I return to the office."

"What about the woman that tried to attack Noreen? The one who threw the knife?"

"She's still sitting in jail."

"Why?" Fenmore asked. She held up her hand and shook her head at Jim. "Sorry, Darius told me what happened with Spencer's shoulder." She turned to the others with a scowl. "I see he wasn't wearing his sling. Let's hope he didn't rip his stitches out when he took Noreen to the ground."

"Shit," Jocelyn said and pulled out her phone. They watched as her fingers flew over the keyboard. "I just sent a text to Noreen." At her look, she shrugged. "I met her at the library, and we got to talking. We exchanged numbers."

"Good," Jim said. "Jennifer Lockwood is still sitting in my jail."

"Why?" they asked as one.

Jim grinned at him. "The judge went out of town for an impromptu fishing trip. He won't be back until Wednesday."

That had the others silent for some time, and the Nash looked at the sheriff with concern. "If she's in jail, does that mean she can't access a phone? Is she married? Dating anyone? Would she know someone that would blame Noreen for getting Jennifer arrested?"

"Where are you going with this?" Simon asked.

"If this was an attack on Noreen, then we're assuming it was Jennifer, but what if it was an attack on Spencer, and Noreen was caught in the crosshairs?"

"Or," Fenmore said. "What if it's against Mattie for doing the firing, and again, Noreen was caught in the crosshairs?"

"First," Jim scowled at the group. "Why would anyone want to go after Barnes?"

"Come on, Jim. The Fuckwad might be in prison, but he still has a long reach. Spencer was the most verbal during his trial, and right in the courtroom, he threatened Spencer. Everyone heard it, and it's even in the court transcript. That's one of the reasons he wasn't granted bail. Not that it's an issue now, but you understand."

"I do," Jim sighed as he rubbed the back of his neck. He shook his head sadly. "Let me see if Gunny has any outside video and take it from there. I'll keep you appraised of the situation."

"If you need our help," Logan said and let the sentence die there. When Jim nodded, they breathed easier. "Let's get this done," Logan looked at the others as he rolled up his sleeves and walked around the SUV. He swore when he saw the damage to both tires. "Whoever did this didn't want Noreen to get very far."

"Maybe they wanted her incapacitated so they could get to her," Simon suggested as he opened the back of the vehicle and began removing the spare tires and the jack. Together the men hunkered down and changed the ruined tires of Noreen's vehicle.

"Everything okay?" Spencer asked after he saw Noreen pull out her phone and look at it. He didn't want to come across as jealous, but it made him curious about who was texting her so late at night."

"Yes, and since we've been honest and upfront with each other all night, I won't stop now. That was Jocelyn."

"You know Jocelyn?"

"I waited on her one day and then saw her at the library. We talked and exchanged numbers. I wouldn't say we're best friends, but we are friends."

"Okay, do you mind if I ask what she wanted?"

"Not at all. My house is just up the road on the left."

Spencer pulled in and looked around. He didn't know if he liked that it was so far back off the road. He would withhold his judgment until he could see it in the daylight. He parked, looked at her with a raised brow, then grinned when she held up her hands. He hurried out of his side of the truck and went around to open the door for her. At the front door, she looked up at him and said, "You're coming inside with me."

"Excuse me?"

"You're coming inside with me. It has nothing to do with sex, at least not now, but Joselyn sent that text to have me check out your shoulder. She and the others are worried that you might have pulled at your stitches when you took us to the ground."

Spencer looked at her in shock and barely noticed when she unlocked her door, grabbed his hand, and pulled him inside her home. The next thing he knew, he was sitting in a chair at the kitchen table with Noreen staring at him with her arms crossed, and she stood there taping her foot.

"What?"

"Take your shirt off. I want to see if you pulled your stitches."

Spencer grinned, then winced as he pulled the shirt he was wearing off his head. He heard a sound and saw Noreen's eyes widen, and she licked her lips at the sight of his bare chest.

"Wow, that's a six-pack."

"Thank you," he grinned, then looked behind Noreen as someone entered the room.

"Mom? What's going on?"

"Chloe, I'd like you to meet Spencer Barnes. This is the gentleman I had a drink with tonight."

"The self-defense guy?"

"Yes," both Noreen and Spencer said at the same time. "We had a little incident at Gunny's. That's why he brought me home."

"What type of incident?"

"Remember I told you Spencer shoved me behind him when Jennifer threw that knife?" She asked her daughter and turned to Spencer. "I don't keep any secrets from my daughter. She should know what's going on."

"I agree. She can be another pair of eyes to keep a lookout."

"What happened?" Chloe demanded.

"When we were in the parking lot ready to leave. Spencer saw something about my truck that didn't look right. He found two of my tires had been slashed."

"Holy crap, two? One I can understand, but why in tarnation would someone want to ruin two of them at once?"

"To keep her immobile," Spencer said. At their looks, he sighed heavily and explained. "In my experience, and I've done this myself on a mission, but in my experience, if you want to capture or harm the owner of the vehicle, you make sure they're stranded. Everyone has a spare, but no one carries around two spare tires. It so happens that your mother does."

"What's this mean? Is someone after her?" Chloe asked in concern as she stood next to her mother.

Spencer smiled when he realized that Chole was a younger version of her mother. They were cut from the same cloth. "We don't know. The sheriff was at the scene when we left, and friends of mine were there. They're changing her tires and will bring the truck here."

"Then why do you have your shirt off? You weren't hoping to get some kitchen table sex, were you?"

"Chloe!" Noreen asked in shock and turned a mean eye on Spencer when he burst out laughing.

"No, at least not yet." He waggled his brows several times. Chloe only rolled her eyes while Noreen turned beet red. "Anyway, if your mother told you what happened to Jennifer, and I saved her from the knife attack, a mutual friend told your mother to see if any of my stitches had pulled apart when I took us both down to the ground."

"First, why would you take Mom to the ground if her tires were slashed? Second, how many stitches are you supposed to have?" She asked this with her nose no more than two inches from the wound. Thankfully, Spencer had a large bandage over it. He reached up to take it off, but she stopped him.

"Let me," she said and went to the sink and washed her hands. That impressed the hell out of him. She turned back and looked at her mother with her hands hovering over the bandage. "Could you please grab the first aid kit?"

Spencer frowned when Noreen turned and hurried away. He looked at Chloe with a raised brow.

"She hates the sight of blood. That's not true; she hates the sight of uncontrolled bleeding. Did that make sense?"

"It did, and it's good to know. Does she faint?"

"No, but she turns green." They chuckled as Chloe removed the bandage, then leaned in close to look at it. "How many?"

"Twenty-seven, both in and out."

After what seemed like hours but only turned into a couple of minutes, Chloe stepped back just as her mother returned with a large blue bag. She set it on the table and looked at Chloe. Spencer also noticed she didn't look at his wound.

"It's good," Chole said and watched as her mother looked. "There aren't any missing or broken stitches, only a little blood. I don't know if it's because of what happened tonight or when this was first done."

She took the items her mother handed her and quickly rebandaged the wound. When the women stepped back from him, Spencer only winced twice as he pulled his shirt back on.

"Tell me," Chloe said as she rewashed her hands and turned to the couple as she dried them. "What else happened to make you concerned about your stitches."

Spencer looked at Noreen, and she only shrugged

at him. He decided to be honest with her like he had been with his mother earlier. Honesty was the best policy in his book. He figured if he wanted a relationship with Noreen, he better establish one with Chloe.

"Someone tried to run us down. We don't know if they were after your mother or me."

"Why? Do you have an ex-wife or ex someone that wants you dead? Are they going after Mom because she's with you?"

"I'm going to go out on a limb and say no to that because I don't have any exes. However, I do have an ex-boss that wants me dead. He's in jail, but that didn't stop him from trying to get to my friends."

"Can I ask what jail?"

"Leavenworth."

"The military jail?"

"Yes."

"Holy crap, he's a bad dude then, right?"

"He is." They paused at the knock on the door, and Noreen when to answer it. She returned with her truck keys and Spencer's friends behind her.

"You okay?" Darius asked as he pointed to Spencer's shoulder.

"He's good," Chloe said. She went to the first one in line and introduced herself. Afterward, she stood beside her mother and asked the room at large. "What's your opinion on what happened?"

"No clue. It could be several things," Nash said.

"Mr. Barnes was telling us it could be his ex-boss coming after him."

"Spencer, please call me Spencer."

"I will," she grinned at him, then turned to the others. "Or, it could be that witch that hates Mom."

"Correct, but she's still in jail with no access to a phone."

"What about any deputies that work at the jail? Could she have played the sad card on one of them and gotten him to make calls for her?" The room became silent, and it was Simon who scowled at her.

"How old are you?"

"Fourteen."

"Damn, we never gave that a thought. We're all going down to talk with the sheriff tomorrow, and we'll mention that to him."

"Will you guys be at the assembly on Friday?"

"No, it'll be just me," Spencer said as he stood. "I hate to drop all this information on you and leave, but your mother has an early shift tomorrow, and you need to get to bed for school."

The others chuckled as Chloe rolled her eyes at him, then said goodbye to the others. After they left, Spencer waited a few minutes and then looked at Noreen. "Walk me out?"

She smiled as she nodded, and together they walked to the front door. When Spencer turned toward her, she shocked him but stood on her toes and kissed him quickly on the corner of his mouth.

He didn't let her go as he turned his head and deepened the kiss. When they broke apart, they were both breathing hard.

"Thank you for saving me."

"You're welcome. Keep my number on you. Better yet, give me your phone, and I'll program it in." They did that for each other, then after a quick kiss on her lips, he looked at her and nodded once. "More of that later. When I leave, don't forget to lock up."

"I won't."

Spencer slipped out the door and waited until he heard the lock click before moving toward his truck and whistling as he left.

CHAPTER 9

SPENCER WALKED down the hall beside the sheriff and the local school's principal. It had been a few days since he had seen Noreen. Not that he didn't want to, but he'd been busy with a new group of people to teach, and her schedule had been all over the place. They had talked every night for the last few nights, and Spencer looked forward to spending time with her and Chloe on Sunday.

He looked up at a commotion ahead of them, quickly pulled out his phone, and began to tape what was happening. The principal left them to hurry over to the action, and the sheriff was beside her.

"At least it wasn't me this time," came a voice from beside him, and Spencer looked down and saw Chloe standing there.

"Does this happen often?"

"Only when Brandi gets a wild hair up her ass

about something." She looked at him and sighed. "Don't tell Mom I swore."

It took everything Spencer had not to bust a gut laughing. "I promise," he said as he nodded to her. Instead of taking them back to the principal's office, they were escorted to the auditorium where the assembly was about to take place. They stood there and watched as the principal and two other teachers broke the students apart.

"Catch you later," Chloe said from his side. By the time Spencer looked down, she was gone. He shook his head with a smile as he rejoined the other two people he had walked up the hall with.

"Before you say anything, I got what happened on video. I'll mention this in my speech, but I hate bullies."

"So do I. I don't know what's come over Brandi lately, but she's in several fights daily. She used to pick fights with Chloe Rafferty, but since Chloe stands her ground, Brandi seems to go after people who are afraid of her."

"What's her home life like?" Spencer asked. He saw the shock on their faces and shrugged. "Seems, from what you described, she's got anger issues. It has to come from somewhere. It makes me wonder what's happening at home, and if she can't do anything there, she's taking that anger out on weaker people here."

"I'll look into it," Principal Black said. They stood

off to the side as students and teachers alike started entering the room. When it looked like most students had arrived, they entered the auditorium. Instead of going up on the stage, Principal Black led them to the area in front of the bleachers where all the students were gathered.

She stood there until it quieted down, then raised her voice for everyone to hear. Spencer estimated that at least seven hundred students were in attendance.

"Thank you for coming," Principal Black began, but someone in the crowd said they had no choice. Black didn't bat an eye.

"You can stay here and listen to what we say or sit in your office, Mr. Wilson." The student body turned, and the boy who called out shook his head.

"I'm good."

"I thought you would be. I called this mandatory assembly for one reason and one reason only. There have been an overwhelming number of bullying claims in recent weeks and months. I brought two gentlemen here today and would like to speak with you. If you listen, that's fine. If you don't, please don't disrupt the people who want to hear what they have to say. With me today are Sheriff Faulker and Mr. Spencer Barnes. I'll let them tell you why they are here. Gentlemen," Black said, then stepped back and sat in the first row, leaving Jim and Spencer standing there.

"Since I'm the sheriff, I can tell you that when Principal Black called me in about her concerns about the bullying around here, I had a horrific thought. Would anyone care to guess what it was?" He asked as he stood there and looked out at the students. Several of them called out things, but he shook his head.

"No, I'll tell you. My thought was that I would have another school shooting on my hands. *I* would be the one to go to your parent's homes and tell them that some of you were dead. *I* would have to be the one that shot one of you because you couldn't handle the abuse from your classmates and went after them —not considering the loss of lives that had nothing to do with why you were bullied or by whom. In my experience, the shooters from those school shootings were someone who was bullied, and when no one did or said anything about it, they went after the people who hurt them. Either physically or emotionally. I won't tolerate that in my county. That is why Principal Black called us in. I'm here to tell you that I will arrest anyone who shows unnecessary force in their bullying. Please don't put it on me to contact your parents that you're either dead or were the cause of other people dying. You don't want to be in jail for the rest of your life." You could hear a pin drop in that room, and Jim turned to Spencer with a nod.

"Your turn." The sheriff walked away, sat next to Principal Black, and gave Spencer another nod.

"Okay, then." Spencer walked to the center of the area and looked at the students staring back at him. He had been apprehensive about how brutally honest he should take his message, but after what Sheriff Faulkner said, he knew he would have to get their attention quickly if he would get his message across to them.

"My name is Master Chief Spencer Barnes. I was in the Navy for twenty-three years, and for the last fifteen of them, I was a member of SEAL Team 6." He paused at the gasps from the students to let what he said sink in. After only a few moments, he stood tall and proud for his following announcement.

"There are two types of people I hate in this world. Those are liars and bullies. In my personal experience, the two go hand in hand. I can't and won't go into any details, but I can tell you this: a person I worked for while on a special military assignment lied and bullied me and several of my buddies. He bullied us so much that he had three of my team members murdered. When we returned stateside from that mission, he continued his lies and bullied us into being discharged from the military. It didn't work. I believe in truth and honesty at all costs."

"What happened next?" Someone called out.

"Well, besides my three buddies being dead, my other teammates and I are free to roam about this great earth and do what we want as long as it's within the law. The bully we worked with, who happened to be a very high-ranking government agency member, is sitting in jail for his lies and the tactics he used that killed my friends." Spencer let that sink in as he walked back and forth before the students, gathering how he would say the next thing on his list.

"I agree with Sheriff Faulkner that if the bullying in this school doesn't stop, you're all heading to another school shooting. It's senseless. If any of you are thinking of coming to school with a gun to take care of the problem, what good will it do if you are dead? Because I can guaran-dam-tee you that you will be shot and killed. If you survive by God's grace, you're looking at jail time for the rest of your life. Again, I ask, what good would that do you? You will forever be labeled as the kid that couldn't hold his shit and went crazy at his school." He stood and watched the students' expressions and nodded when he saw understanding in them.

"Next, we have the bullies that pushed the shooter to act out." Spencer looked around and walked down the line to stop before a girl he had videoed earlier. "You, what's your name?"

"Brandi, with an 'i'."

"Oh, you're one of those," Spencer said snidely and stepped back so he could see everyone at once. "I want to conduct a little experiment here. I want people to stand if I call out a name. It can be any variation of the name I'm calling out. Brandi, Jennifer,

Amber, Ashley, Jessica, Justin, Jason, Brandon, and Tyler." Spencer watched as at least two hundred kids stood. "Okay, now, this next question is aimed at you people. Earlier today, I witnessed some bullying in the hallway. I caught it on my phone, and you can bet that I will contact your parents to address this issue. My question is this, what makes you think you're so special?"

"Why are you asking that?" Principal Black asked in general confusion.

"Because as I walked through the halls, I over-heard several students talking that there was some club, and to become a member, you had to have one of those names. Which is stupid, but Brandi, what makes you so special? Is it because you have an 'i' in your last name? That just means your parents didn't know how to spell." He saw anger come over the girl's face and shrugged. "Get angry. I don't care. Young kids today are spineless twits, so I blame your parents. Why? Because they are the ones that should have taught you manners and instilled those into you. It's not the job of the teachers to do that. The teacher's jobs are to teach you the basic skills to survive in the world, which include reading, writing, and math. Anything above and beyond that is all a luxury that kids today take for granted. You shouldn't." He looked around and nodded. "Please, you can resume your seat." He waited until they sat, then strolled before them again.

"I know I will get many angry parents contacting me, but you know what? I don't give a shit. If they had taught you right from the beginning, we wouldn't be here talking about bullying and the possible ramifications if someone goes on a rampage to get revenge. It's not worth it. I know. I've been all over the world and seen and experienced the horrific aftermath of that anger. What I just said to you was to back up what Sheriff Faulkner said about the possibility of having a school shooting here. We both don't want that to happen, and I can bet you don't either.

"Before I get to why Principal Black invited me to talk today, I want to say this. If you are being a bully, I implore you to get help. Talk to someone, whether it's a friend, a teacher, or a counselor. Write your feelings down in a journal, but talk to someone. Again, because of my personal experience, there are some underlying issues about why you are being a bully.

"Second, I hate using the word victim, but if you are one of the students being bullied, I also implore you to talk with someone. This leads me to why I am here. As I said, my name is Master Chief Barnes, and I have decades of experience as a military man. My friends and I, who had been bullied out of our careers, moved here to Fool's Gold to open a facility to help others. Not only in this community, but we've helped former and current military personnel, police, and even FBI agents. We work up at The Centre. I am personally responsible for the self-defense and martial arts program. I can teach you how to defend yourself against a bully that doesn't involve putting your hands on them. That's assault, and they can press charges against you." Spencer looked directly at Brandi as he said, "What you did earlier is also considered assault, and the person you shoved around can press charges against you. You can bet I'll talk with your victim and her parents."

"What about using your words?" A student called out.

"That's stupid and asinine," Spencer said. "What good do words do if someone's beating your ass? Was I supposed to use my words when I had a suicide bomber coming at me? I'm not saying you should fight violence with violence, but you can learn how to defend yourself against bullies. Again, my personal experience says that if someone is only verbally abusing you now, it will almost always escalate into physical violence. Abuse is abuse, no matter if it's verbal, physical, or even mental. Also, no matter how old or big you are, you must recognize the signs of abuse and protect yourself against it." He looked at the students and shook his head when he decided to tell them the next part.

"Look at me. I am a six-foot, four-inch man that weighs around two hundred and twenty pounds. I have twenty-three years of military experience under my belt. As I told you at the beginning of my speech, someone lied about me and bullied my buddies and me out of our careers. It doesn't matter how big you are. Anyone can be bullied. The person who did this to us happened to be high up in the government food chain." Spencer shook his head and held up his hand as he saw several hands from the students shoot up. "No, I will not give more details than I already did. The only other thing I can say is that this person is in jail while we are not. The higher-ups in the military are investigating the lies he told them." He walked back and forth again and knew the kids wanted to ask questions, but he wasn't at liberty to answer them. Add the fact that he didn't think he had to answer to children for the Fuckwad's actions.

"Okay, then. Your teachers are handing out a flyer for you to take home and discuss with your parents. It's a little bit of what I offer up at The Centre. I teach self-defense classes for both adults and students. I also teach Martial Arts for the same. If you're interested, call the number on the flyer, and we can set up an appointment for you and your parents to come in and talk about it. Since most of you are under eighteen, I will need your parents' signatures before you start your first class. Also, keep in mind that we can work on a sliding scale, and we do take payments." Spencer watched as the stacks of flyers he'd brought with him were being passed from one student to the next, and he nodded when he saw the students tuck them in a pocket or backpack. He didn't say anything else until the last person had a flyer, then spoke loud and clear.

"Other than my problem with the bully I mentioned earlier, does anyone have any questions?"

"I do," Brandi jumped to her feet, cocker her hip, and Spencer only looked at her with a raised brow. Her body language screamed 'attitude' to him—something he wouldn't tolerate.

"Yes?"

"Why did you take a videotape of what happened earlier?"

"Because of my experience with the bully, I mentioned. He lied to us and then falsified the information to suit his needs. That is not the truth. If I have an opportunity to get someone's bad actions on tape, then the person being harmed has the proof of what happened to them." He stood there with his arms crossed and had a staring contest with her. She never backed down until he asked his next question.

"Without the video I took, which I will give to the girl's parents. But, without that video, would you have admitted it if she came forward with allegations of you pushing her around?"

Brandi glared at him, then sat back down without answering him. "I thought not." Spencer looked around and asked if there were any other questions. When he did that, Sheriff Faulkner and Principal Black rejoined him. The three answered questions for the next twenty minutes. The principal concluded the assembly with the consequences to the bullies if the behavior continued and what actions the school would take to ensure the safety of the entire student body. Spencer stood right where he was when the students were dismissed. It shocked him when several boys came up and asked him about his military career.

"As much as we want to know what happened," one boy said. "We respect your wishes. I want to know how hard it is to become a SEAL?"

"Hard," Spencer said, then laughed. "A motto of a SEAL is, 'The only hard day was yesterday.' This is true. You never know what the day will bring, and if you are mentally and physically trained, you can handle anything."

"How can we train physically?" Another student asked.

"Do you have a bus to catch?"

"No, we walk."

"Okay, if you want to start training physically, get with your gym coach. Start trying out for sports. If you want to do it on your own, start jogging. Did you take a flyer that was passed out?"

"Yes."

"Go home, read it over. Look us our website. Talk it over with your parents, and come up and talk with us. We can head you in the right direction."

"Are your buddies also SEALS?"

"No, there are three former Delta Force soldiers and one Ranger."

"Damn," the third boy said. "Sorry, Principal Black," he said sheepishly when she reprimanded him for swearing. "Those are the best of the best."

"We are. Take the flyer home, talk with your parents, then come see us." Spencer pulled his wallet out, then withdrew three business cards. He gave them to the boys with a nod. "That's my direct line at The Centre. Give me a call, I'll be in and out of my office, but I'll answer any questions you have."

"But not about what happened."

"Correct." Spencer respected the boys when they held out their hands to shake his, and after they walked away, he turned to the principal. "Are they good students?"

"They are, but I fear they are the victims of bullies. I don't have any proof, but there are rumors that they get pushed around if they don't "help" other students with their homework. I used the air quotes because the help the bullies want is to have those boys do their work for them, then allow them to copy off their tests."

"I understand," Spencer said and looked up when he saw someone out of the corner of his eye. As much as he wanted to approach Chloe, he didn't know how she would react to him seeking her out, so he waited to see what she would do. He didn't know if it surprised him when she approached him and held out her hand.

"That was a great talk, Mr. Barnes. I must say, I loved how you put Brandi in her place."

"This student," Principal Black turned to Spencer with a smile and a look of pride. "This is Chloe Rafferty. She came to me when bullied and stuck up for herself against Brandi. Because of her, those other students came forward, and we realized we had such a huge problem. As the sheriff said, we don't want another school shooting on our hands, and we're trying everything in our power to get a handle on the bullying and keep our students safe."

"That's good to hear," Spencer said, not knowing what else to say. "Has it helped with the bullying?"

"Yes, Brandi's moved onto someone else, but you caught her in the act and called her out. I don't know if it did any good or if she'll continue but be worse than before."

"If you need someone to talk to, you can call me," Spencer said as he handed her a business card. She thanked him and quickly left, saying she had a bus to catch. With the three of them left in the auditorium, they looked at each other, but before Spencer said what was on his mind, Principal Black spoke.

"Thank you both for being brutally honest with them. You are both outside people, and I like that you have some hard truths. As the principal and teachers, we must watch how we speak to the students. Whether it helped or not will remain to be seen."

"Can I ask you one thing?" Spencer spoke as they headed toward the exit.

"What's that?"

"What's up with Brandi? I'm not familiar with teenagers, but that chick has some attitude on her."

"Yeah, she does. I have no clue what happened. She and Chloe were like two peas in a pod until they returned from Christmas break. She's been bullying everyone, acting out, and she's on the verge of failing. She used to be an A student."

"What's her last name?" Jim asked, and when he wrote it down, he nodded and shrugged. "I'll see if there have been any domestic calls to her home. I can't tell you if there have been, but I can look into it."

"Thank you, Jim. As I said, Brandi used to be a great kid, but lately, along with her attitude, is this sense of deep-rooted anger. I have no clue where it's coming from." They walked out onto the sidewalk together and watched as students boarded buses, got into cars, or started walking down the street. Spencer didn't leave until the last bus pulled out, then he walked to his truck and headed to The Centre.

CHAPTER 10

SPENCER PULLED into his parking space and quickly
exited his vehicle. He paused when someone called
his name and grinned as the mailman approached
him.

"Hal, how are you doing today?"

"Good. I have a certified letter here for you to
sign for." Hal shoved the envelope and a clipboard in
his hand, and without looking at the letter, Spencer
signed his name, then took the rest of the mail from
Hal. They said their goodbyes, and he went back to
the building to his office. By the time he sorted the
mail, he had forgotten the letter he'd signed until he
reached the bottom of the pile.

Spencer picked it up and scowled when he read
the return address. He carefully slit it open, treating
it like it might explode at any second. When nothing
happened, he withdrew the single sheet of paper and

read it. He sat there in stunned silence for a long time. After re-reading the letter for what had to have been the fifth time, he jumped to his feet and ran down the hall.

"What the hell?" Nash asked as Spencer burst into the break room and almost took the other man out. "Are you okay?"

"No, where are the others?"

"Finishing up classes or in their offices, why?"

"I want an emergency meeting."

Nash only stared at him with raised brows but went over to the wall and hit the button that gave the other's phone a silent alarm. It was a signal they had come up with when they all had to be together at once. It took ten minutes for them all to arrive.

"What's up?" Darius asked as he retrieved a bottle of water from the refrigerator and sat at the table.

Spencer didn't waste any time as he turned to the other man and demanded. "Did you know?"

"Know what?"

"Did Fenmore tell you anything?" Instead of waiting for an answer, Spencer walked over to the table to throw the letter he had clenched in his fists at the other man. He watched Darius intently as he picked it up, smoothed it out, then read it. As soon as Darius looked at him in shock, he knew Darius didn't know anything, causing Spencer to breathe easier.

Not waiting to be told what was happening, Logan reached across the table and grabbed the letter. As he read, Simon and Nash read over his shoulder. They all looked at Spencer at the same time, then at Darius.

"What the fuck does this mean?"

"No clue, but I understand that if the Fuckwad is convicted, then we have a chance of getting our discharge overturned in our favor." Spencer grinned, and the others reared back from the evil look on his face. "This is perfect."

"Why?" Nash asked as he settled back in his chair.

"We all know the Fuckwad hated us for, as he told the courts at our trials, coming out smelling like roses. He was jealous because we got the job done and made him look bad. Wouldn't it be great if they overturned our other-than-honorary discharge into an honorary one, and we could get all our benefits back? Or VA benefits, our pensions, everything. I think if this happens, then this will be our final fuck you to the Fuckwad for thinking he could ruin us."

Spencer watched as the four men sat there in stunned silence, then a slow grin came over their faces. "I like what you're saying, but I'm not going to get my hopes up," Simon said. "I only have one question."

"What's that?"

"Why do you have this letter and not us?"

"I met Hal outside when I came back from school. He said I had a certified letter. I don't know about you guys, but until everyone the Fuckwad hired to come after us is caught, I have all my mail delivered here. I don't have a PO Box or mailbox at my apartment."

"Wow, I never thought of that," Simon said. "That was smart, so we might have something when we get home?"

"Or a card to tell you to go to the post office to sign for it."

"I had a thought," Logan scowled at them. When he had their attention, he shook his head continuously. "The letter's fine and good, but you know how slow the military works when it comes to them fixing their mistakes. With that said, I've been thinking about what happened to your woman's vehicle."

"And?" The others asked as one.

"What if the Fuckwad *did* send someone after you. He went after Darius, Simon, and Nash. You must be next on his list."

"How did they know about Noreen?" Spencer asked in confusion. "I understand what you're saying, but I don't think it's that. My being with Noreen that night was our first time together."

"What if someone's watching us? Could they have been in the diner when that other chick was arrested and tried to go after her, but you stepped in to stop the knife aimed at Noreen?"

"Shit," they all said as they settled back in their chairs and lost themselves in their thoughts.

"Do you still have the video you took at the restaurant?" Simon asked.

"I do."

"Put it on the big screen, and maybe we can have a wider focus of the area." Spencer did as asked, then they sat back and watched it. They viewed it several times before Simon called out to have the tape paused.

"I'll be a son-of-a-bitch," he said as he jumped and went to the wall where they had projected the video. "There isn't a way to zoom out, is there?"

"I'll try," Spencer did, and they were allotted only a few more inches of video. It was enough to have Simon swearing as he pointed to the image before them.

"What is it?"

"That's the guy that shot Jocelyn and me outside a restaurant. It's the guy Swede was able to uncover information on."

"Who is he?" Spencer asked and shook his head. As he looked up, Simon had disappeared, only to return on a dead run minutes later, holding a file. He flipped it open and pointed to the photo there.

"Nate Renaldo. I recognized the tattoo on his forearm. Swede from the Brotherhood Protection Agency uncovered that he is a Syrian Insurgent the Fuckwad hired to take us out on that last mission. They only succeeded in getting three of us. Last I heard, he hadn't been caught yet. If he was in the diner, he knew you protected Noreen, and he must have waited to see what she drove, then followed her."

"Shit," Spencer said, grabbing the photo to study it intently. The five of them looked up in confusion when they heard a commotion at the front of the building. Before they could investigate, a man came barreling with Deputy Sheriff Sparrow down the hall.

"Which one of you is the perverted fuckhead here?"

"Huh?" The five men said as one.

"Who are you?" Spencer demanded and stepped back when the man tried to take a swing at him. Darius and Simon got to him before Sparrow did, and they had him jacked up against the wall so he wouldn't take another swing at them.

"What's going on?" Spencer demanded as he stood to his height of well over six feet, towering over the other man.

Sparrow sighed as she rubbed her forehead and shook her head. "This is Tom Dickson, and he called the station to say he was coming here to kill someone. I only got about every tenth word before he hung up on me."

"Now," Nash said as he stepped up to the man. "You will conduct yourself calmly and tell us why you are so bent on hurting someone.

Tom looked around wildly, and he must have

realized he couldn't do what he wanted, so he sighed heavily and slumped against the wall. Darius let him go but didn't step too far away from him.

"Well?" Nash asked when Tom didn't speak right away.

"Fine, my little girl came home from school today and said a man took a video of her in a compromising position. When I pressed further, she only said he worked here." He glared at each man in turn, then turned to Sparrow. "I want these sick fucks arrested for taking those videotapes."

"What's you're daughter's name?" Spencer asked though he thought he knew who it was.

"Brandi Dickson. She's only fourteen years old." Tom slumped further, and the look he turned on them had Spencer's gut-wrenching in anguish with him.

"I won't sugar coat anything here, Mr. Dickson. It was me. I took the video, but before you get your panties in a twist again, you need to know that Sheriff Jim Faulkner was standing beside me when I took it. We were at the school today for an assembly. When we left there, I came here, and the sheriff was going to someone's house to show them that video."

"Why would he do that? Brandi told me she was caught in a compromising position." Tom looked genuinely confused. They all watched as Spencer strode over to where his phone was already hooked to the computer. After fiddling with several buttons, he looked over at Tom.

"Are you sure you want to see this? Brandi was correct in what she told you. She was caught in a compromising position, but it's not what you think it is. If the other parents decided to press charges against your daughter, she could face assault charges."

"What the fuck?" Tom demanded as he shoved himself off the wall and approached the table. Darius and Simon were on either side of him. Before Spencer played the video in question, he scowled at Tom.

"Question, do you know a girl named Chloe Rafferty?"

"Yes, she's been Brandi's best friend since she moved here years ago. Almost ten years."

"Correct, according to Ms. Chloe, and I have reason to think she would lie to me, but according to her, they haven't been best friends since they returned to school after the Christmas break. I have no clue what happened, nor is it any of my business. I know that you need to get to the bottom of what I'm about to show you, or you'll have bigger problems than your daughter lying to you about being video-taped in a compromising position. The only thing I can think of is that she told you what she did because she probably expected you to get this tape and destroy it without watching it."

"I'm not going to watch my daughter if she's naked," Tom yelled at him.

"Watch," Spencer said as he fiddled with the controls, then pointed to the wall. Everyone turned to view what was playing, and Spencer kept his eye on Tom. He saw his buddies raise their brows out of the corner of his eye, and Sparrow scowled at the screen. She was the one that demanded he plays it again. After the third time, Spence turned to Tom and only raised a brow at him.

"Fuck me," Tom said as he scrubbed his face.

"Not my type," Spencer said, not missing a beat, and Tom shook his head at him. "I'm sorry for coming at you as I did, and I will get to the bottom of this. You say Chloe said Brandi was like this after the Christmas Break?"

"Yes, I don't know what type of person your daughter was before then, but Ms. Rafferty told me that she went to the principal because when she wouldn't allow Brandi to copy off her test, Brandi did to Chloe what you so her do on the video to this other girl. Sir, I may be stepping out of line here, but something happened, and your daughter is taking her anger issues out on her friends. I'm not the police or a counselor, but I suggest you help her."

"What do you do here?"

Logan stepped forward then and told him what they all offered, and he looked Tom dead in the eye as he said his next piece. "I'm not a parent, but I think

Spencer's self-defense and martial arts classes might work for Brandi, but not before she controls her anger issues. For that, I think she might benefit from Nash's yoga classes. Not to be a bastard, but Nash is the most Zen mother fucker I've ever met. His calmness might rub off onto your daughter."

"But not before you find out what her deal is," Nash said as he shook his head at the group. "No amount of calmness and Zen will help if you don't know what will trigger her anger. From what I saw on that tape, your daughter has serious anger issues. I'd look into it if I were you."

"Where do I even begin?"

"I have a suggestion," Spencer said. "You probably won't like it, but it's the only thing I can think of off the top of my head."

"What is it? I'm spinning out here, wondering where the hell to start."

"Does Brandi have any siblings?"

"Yes, and older brother and sister."

"Are they in college or live away from home? Did they bring someone home with them over the holidays and do something to Brandi? Could they have threatened her that if she told anyone, then they would harm her sibling? You know, the one that brought them home?"

"Shit, they both brought friends home. I'll look into it." Tom barely had the statement out of his mouth before he turned on his heel and disappeared through the doorway. Sparrow looked at the men with raised brows, shook her head, and hurried after him. When they were left alone again, they looked at one another with raised brows.

"Wow."

"Yeah."

CHAPTER 11

Noreen stumbled into the kitchen on Sunday morning, yawning and barely opening her eyes. Yesterday she had worked the entire time the diner had been open. With Jennifer gone, it put pressure on the other staff until Mattie could hire someone new. Oh, don't get her wrong; she loved the tips, but it had been hell with all her walking. She shuffled to the coffee pot and smiled when a cup of the steaming brew was held out to her.

"Thanks," Noreen whispered to her daughter as she cradled the cup in her hands, brought it to her face, and sniffed the fragrant brew. After taking a tentative sip, she closed her eyes to savor both the flavor and the fragrance. Once she had her third sip, she opened her eyes and smiled at Chloe. "Morning."

"Morning," Chloe laughed at her mother. "Would

you like a bagel? That's what I'm having for breakfast."

"You don't want anything more?"

"No, the bagel will be enough."

"Sure, I'll take one." Noreen settled in her chair at the table to sip her coffee and watched as her daughter prepared both bagels and poured them a small glass of juice each. Neither of them said a word as they ate their breakfast. When they did speak, it was Chloe who spoke first.

"Do you have to work today?"

"No, it's my normal day off. I worked a double yesterday because Mattie hasn't hired someone yet to replace Jennifer."

"Do you think she'll ever come back? Jennifer, I mean?"

"No, she was fired for stealing. Get this," Noreen said as she rose from her chair and went over to the table near the back door. She picked up her work apron and brought it back to the table. Without saying a word, she shoved it toward her daughter. "I didn't count it last night. I was too busy, then too tired once I got home. That's all my tips from yesterday."

Chloe frowned but pulled the apron toward her. "It's heavier than usual."

"I know. I suspected Jennifer was stealing my tips but couldn't prove it. Mr. Barnes happened to see her do it the other day, and he taped her doing it. Jennifer couldn't deny why she was fired because it was on video, and one of the other witnesses was Sheriff Faulkner."

"Holy crap," Chloe looked at her mother with wide eyes. Together they counted the money Noreen had made the day before. "One question. Is this what you would normally make in a day?"

"I'd say half that because I worked a double yesterday, but yes, I'd bring home most of what is here when Jennifer wasn't working. When she was working, I'd barely bring home twenty dollars."

"I'm glad she was fired." Chloe nodded and proceeded to count the money before her. She grinned at her mother and had to wait for her to sit back down after refilling her coffee cup.

"Why the grin?"

"If all our bills are paid, and this is extra money, then we have enough for both of us to sign up for those self-defense classes."

"Really?" Noreen looked at her daughter in shock. She quickly grabbed the stack of bills and counted it. With a grin, she looked at her daughter. "Well, since I invited Mr. Barnes to spend the day with us, I will talk to him about the classes."

"Whoo Hoo!" Chloe yelled, surprising her mother, then did a happy dance in her seat. She stared at her mother in shock, then laughed as she jumped to her feet and ran away. She returned in under three minutes. She did something with her phone, and after taking several deep breaths to calm herself, she looked at her mother. "Remember we had the assembly on Friday?"

"Yes, what was it about?"

"The bullying going on at school. Sheriff Faulkner spoke, then Mr. Barnes made a speech. I taped it." She grinned as she turned her phone to show her mother. "Press play." Chloe moved her chair so she could rewatch it while her mother watched it for the first time.

"Oh, my," Noreen said at the beginning of Spencer's speech, then didn't say anything until the very end. "He's dynamic when he speaks. Something about him tells me that what he said was the absolute truth."

"Yeah, me too. I don't think he is the type of person that would tell lies. I particularly like the part where he put Brandi in her spot. I didn't video it, but I saw something before the assembly started that made my opinion of Mr. Barnes rise several notches."

"What was that?" Noreen asked as she sipped her coffee.

"Brandi was bullying another girl in the hallway. Mr. Barnes saw it, and he used his phone to tape it. As soon as he did, Principal Black, the Sheriff, and three other teachers were right there to help Heather. Brandi had to sit next to Principal Black during the assembly."

"Wow, is that why he called her out?"

DEANNA L. ROWLEY

"Yes." Chloe looked at her mother and rolled her eyes. "I can only imagine what Brandi will tell her parents. Knowing her, she'll probably spin it to get Mr. Barnes in trouble or something stupid, like to have him arrested."

Noreen shrugged and shook her head. "I have no clue what will happen. Anyway, how about helping me with the housework until Mr. Barnes arrives?"

"I cleaned yesterday while you were at work. We only have to clean up from breakfast, and you have to do your laundry. I did mine yesterday."

Noreen reached over, gripped her daughter's head in her hands, and kissed her forehead. "Thank you. While you do that, I'll go gather my laundry. What do you want for supper?"

"Can you teach me how to make lasagna? I got the meat out of the freezer yesterday, and we have all the other ingredients." Chloe's cheeks turned pink as she looked at her mother. "I looked at your recipe to make sure we had everything."

"And if we didn't have it?"

"I was going to send you a text last night to see if you could stop at the store on your way home. Since we had everything, I didn't."

"You are such a great kid," Noreen said as she walked over and gave her a hug.

"Mom," Chloe complained after giving her mother a quick hug, then she tried to push her away.

Laughing, Noreen left the kitchen. For the first

time in a long time, she had some pep in her step and felt great. She couldn't wait to teach her daughter how to make lasagna from scratch.

SPENCER PACED in his small apartment, running his hands through his hair and repeatedly turning in circles. "Fuck it," he said as he grabbed his truck keys and left home. He was supposed to meet with Noreen that day, and they hadn't put an exact time on the date. He had been up and anxious to get to her house since six that morning. He hurried down the stairs and out to his truck with his keys in his hand. He drove by remotely to her house and hadn't even looked at the time until he pulled into the driveway. It was almost ten thirty, but he shrugged as he exited his truck, pocketed his keys, and walked to the front door.

Before Spencer could knock, the door opened, and Chloe stood there with a gigantic grin on her face.

"Mr. Barnes, welcome."

"Spencer, please."

"Okay, Spencer, it is then, welcome." The girl stepped back to let Spencer enter, and he looked at her feet, then pointed to his own. "Do you want my shoes off or on?"

"It's up to you, Mom and I are in our slippers, but you can keep them on if you want to."

Spencer shook his head as he bent down to untie his combat boots, then set them beside the door. When he was done, he looked at Chloe with a grin. "Lead the way."

"Oh, sorry, I don't think I've ever seen shoes that big before. If it's not too rude of me, what size are they?"

"Sixteen," Spencer said and stopped behind Chloe when he caught sight of Noreen standing at the kitchen island with a small card in her hand. She looked up and gave him a sweet smile, which Spencer felt go directly to his cock. He hoped he wouldn't embarrass himself with his instant erection at seeing the beautiful woman before him.

"Mr. Barnes, welcome."

"Spencer, please call me Spencer."

"Okay, Spencer. Welcome."

"I hope I'm not too early?"

"Not at all. We hadn't really set a time for you to come over. I hope you don't mind, but we're having lasagna for dinner tonight. I'm about to show Chloe how to make it. From scratch."

"Oh wow, can I watch?"

"You can help," Chloe said, looking at her mother with a grin. "Why don't you tell Spencer and me what to do?"

"That sounds like fun," Spencer said as he went to

the kitchen and washed his hands in the sink. He grinned at her as he dried them on the towel Noreen handed him. If he hadn't been studying her so intently, he never would have seen her swallow hard, or heard her moan. He grinned harder. *This was going to be fun,* he thought to himself.

"I don't know," Noreen hesitated but looked at her daughter when she snorted a laugh.

"Mom, how am I going to learn if I don't do it myself? You know I learn better with hands-on. Besides, you worked all day yesterday. Sit down, and let Spencer and I cook. I'll even clean up the mess afterward."

"I'll help." Spencer volunteered.

"Fine," Noreen said as she refilled her coffee cup and took a seat facing them. "How much from scratch do you want to do this?"

"What's that mean?" Spencer asked as he looked between Noreen and Chloe. When Chloe wore the expression he felt he had, they both turned to Noreen.

"I mean, do you want to make the sauce from scratch? Or do you want to use bottled?"

"Scratch," both Spencer and Chloe said at the same time. Spencer went to the refrigerator, and before he opened it, he looked at the others with raised brows. After getting permission, he opened it and began bringing out several items. At one point, he looked at Chloe. "Garlic?"

He nodded when the girl opened the freezer and brought it out. With the items lined up on the counter, they looked at Noreen for directions. For the next few hours, the three of them cooked, talked, laughed, and got to know one another. Spencer couldn't remember the last time he had so much fun in the kitchen. It wasn't that he didn't know how to cook. He did. His mother made sure of that while he'd been growing up. It was just that he didn't always cook for himself because cooking for one sucked. Since moving to Fool's Gold, he's found that he ate most of his meals either at the diner or over at Gunny's.

HOURS LATER, Noreen pushed her plate away, sighed happily, then reached for her wine glass. She had just finished her second plate of the lasagna Spencer and Chloe had made per her instructions and was now a full and content woman.

"I think," she mumbled into her wine glass. She took a sip as the others looked at her, and with a grin, she continued, "I think, Chloe, from now on, you're in charge of making the lasagna."

"Only if Spencer makes the sauce," Chloe said cheekily as she grinned at Spencer. "He was the one that made the sauce, if. If I recall correctly, I only got the ingredients and handed them to him as he added them. This was awesome."

"Thank you," Spencer took his praise and saluted the two with his own glass of wine. "I only have one question for you."

"What's that?"

"Do you make that homemade sauce just for the lasagna? Or do you do it for all your pasta dishes?"

"Usually, I only do it for the lasagna, and I only cook that dish when I have time."

"We need to bottle that sauce," Chloe said as she began stacking the dishes. She had the forethought while she and Spencer had been cooking to clean as they went, so the only dishes they had to clean now were the ones they ate off of.

"It would go bad before we could use it," Noreen said as she settled back into her seat.

"No, it wouldn't," Spencer said from his position at the sink, filling it with hot soapy water. "There is a way to do it. I'd have to call my mother and ask her, but while I was growing up, Mom was forever putting things in jars to preserve them. We had a huge garden, and I think what she did was called canning."

"It is," Chloe said as she looked up from her phone and showed her mother. "There's even a YouTube video on how to do it."

Noreen took the phone with a laugh, then watched the video as the other two cleaned up. She handed the phone back, and when Spencer asked if she wanted more wine, she declined. Once the kitchen was put back to rights, they gravitated toward the living room. Noreen and Spencer sat side by side on the sofa while Chloe sat across the room. It was several minutes before any of them spoke.

"Chloe, could I ask you something?" Spencer asked, and when Chloe turned her whole attention on him, he knew he would get a straight answer.

"Sure, what's up?"

"Friday, after I got back to my office from the assembly, a few hours later, Brandi's father came storming in demanding whom the pervert was that taped his daughter in a compromising position."

"Let me guess, Brandi told her father that to try to get you into trouble?"

"I think so, and I also think she tried to get that video I took back so her parents wouldn't know what she did."

"It's just her father. Her mother left last year. One day she was there. The next, she was gone. No one knows why. She does have an older brother and sister, but they're away at different colleges. What happened?"

"After we calmed him down, I showed him the video. I asked if he knew you, and he said you were Brandi's best friend. I hope I didn't overstep, but I told him that hadn't been the case since Christmas. That is what he saw his daughter do to that girl she had done to you. I could see genuine shock and concern on his face. I asked if anyone had been there at the time of her change and did something to her or threatened her."

"I can see that," Chloe said as she swung her legs to the floor and looked at Spencer. "That might be why she's acting out. She has something to say but can't talk to anyone for fear of it getting back to the person who might have threatened her and something happening."

"That's what I thought. I don't know the entire story, but is there any way you could reach out to her? Maybe as a former friend, she would open up to you. Or did Brandi burn her bridges with you?"

"No, there's still some rope left there. She didn't hang herself completely. I understand what you're asking, but I'd have to think about it for a couple of days."

"Okay," Spencer shrugged. "I was only asking, not like demanding you to reach out to her. After seeing her in action at the assembly, I completely understand if you don't want to reach out to her."

"It's not that I don't want to. It's just that I have to thicken my skin in order to talk to her."

They left it at that, and within half an hour, Chloe excused herself, saying she was going up to her room.

"Thank you," Noreen said quietly several minutes later.

"For?"

"Asking Chloe to reach out to Brandi. Brandi is a great kid. I would hate to see her fall through the cracks if something happened to her, and she's angry because of it."

Spencer shrugged as he turned to look at Noreen and sucked in his breath at her beauty.

"I probably should be getting home," Spencer said sadly but perked up at her next words.

"You don't have to."

CHAPTER 12

"What did you say?" Spencer asked, hopeful he had heard her correctly.

"You don't have to leave yet if you don't want to. It's still early. Unless you have someplace you need to be?"

"Nope, not until I report to work in the morning."

"Me too. What time do you half to report in?"

"Eight. You?"

"I'm mid-shift tomorrow. That means I go in at ten to help with the last of the breakfast crowd, work for the lunch crowd, then start on the supper. I'm supposed to be done at six, but I've been filling in hours since Mattie fired Jennifer."

"I'm so sorry about that. I didn't think my speaking up would have caused others any harm."

"No harm, I've just been busy, and it proved my point."

"Which was?"

"With Jennifer gone, my tips have almost tripled. That tells me she has been stealing them for a while now. With me working a double yesterday, Chloe and I came to a decision. With yesterday's tips, we will be able to both take your self-defense classes."

"Great, when you get some time, come on up to The Centre, and we can fill out the paperwork. I don't have my schedule with me, nor is it memorized, but I'm sure we can come up with something to work around your work."

"How many times a week are the classes?"

"You can take either one or two a week. It all depends on your schedule. The only day I'm not available is Sunday. That's the only day I have off. I do have martial arts classes on Saturdays." He looked at her with a grin. "It's the five to seven crowd."

"Come again?"

"Five-years-old to seven-years-old."

"Oh, wow, they must be cute to watch."

Spencer laughed as he settled back into the couch. "They are, but they're little devil demons at times. The hardest part I'm having right now is trying to drill into them that they aren't supposed to use the moves they learn on their siblings or classmates. They can practice and use them during class, but not on others."

Noreen started to stifle her giggle, but it turned into a full-blown laugh when she pictured what he had said. "Sorry, it's just that I pictured you standing there in your white outfit, with a black belt, and the kids you're glaring down at don't quite reach your knee. I guess I would call them ankle biters."

Spencer stared at her in shock, then as he pictured it, he threw his head back and laughed. "Yeah, I can see that." It took them several moments to get themselves under control. Then Spencer turned to her. He hadn't realized how close he was until his nose brushed her cheek. It didn't take much for him to move just right, and his lips locked onto hers.

It was several minutes before they broke apart, and when they did, Spencer laid his forehead on hers and sighed heavily, but contently. "I'm not going to apologize for that. It was wonderful."

"I agree. I'm not normally this forward, but do you have any condoms on you?"

"I do."

"Good. Do you want to join me upstairs? Before you answer that, I'm going to warn you that it's been a long, long time since I've been with anyone, and I probably forgot how to do things. I don't want you to hold it against me."

"I won't, and if that kiss was any indication, you haven't forgotten a thing. I have to warn you, too. It's been about four years for me. What I'm about to say isn't to get you to change your mind. I want to put my cards on the table from the beginning." When she nodded, he drew in a deep breath, let it out in a rush, and said, "In the past, I only hooked up with women for a one-and-done deal. I've never had any type of relationship that lasted more than one night. There's something about you that tells me I want more. If we go upstairs, I *will* be contacting you again. Are we moving too fast? Probably, but I want you. I have since I saw you across the diner last week. I can't get you out of my thoughts." He grinned when she threw herself against him, and he caught her in time for them to lock lips.

They stayed that way for several minutes until Spencer put a halt to it. "Where's your room?"

"Upstairs, first door on left." Noreen gave a squeak, then a giggle, when he quickly stood, picked her up in his arms, and strode toward where he thought the stairs were. He glowered at him when she giggled harder and pointed in the other direction. He turned on his heel and strode to where she'd pointed. Taking the stairs two at a time, he quickly found the door he wanted. He only waited long enough for her to reach down and open the door before he strode inside, turned, and used his elbow to shut the door. With her still in his arms, he looked around, nodded once, then strode toward the bed. He looked at her with a grin, held her out over the center of the bed, then unceremoniously dumped her in the middle of it. Before she could say anything, he followed her down and covered her lips with his.

"Holy shit," Noreen said several minutes later as she broke off the kiss to try to catch her breath. "You know how to kiss."

"Thank you, want to see what else I know how to do?" He asked as he made his brows go up and down. Noreen couldn't help it. She laughed.

"Sure, what do you have?" She looked at him with a grin, then had to suck in her breath when he rose up to his knees and removed his shirt. The only time Noreen had ever seen a man with a body like Spencer's was on TV or the cover of the romance novels she loved to read. Unable to resist, she sat up and reached for him. When she touched his shoulder, she looked at his expression and didn't know if she should be worried or not when he closed his eyes. When he didn't stop her, she continued her exploration of his body. At one point, she stopped when he made a funny sound. The look on his face was a mixture of pain and pleasure. Shortly after that, she followed her hands with her mouth. She kissed her way across his impressive chest, down his abs, but when she reached the waistband of his jeans, he stopped her.

"Not yet," he said in a strained voice. "My turn." He looked at her and quickly removed her shirt, leaving her bra on. With Spencer hoovering over her, Noreen laid back down and looked up at him. She smiled encouragement and sighed in relief when he laid down next to her, laid one hand on her stomach, and leaned down to kiss her. The next thing Noreen knew, she was naked, and Spencer was poised over her.

"You take my breath away," she murmured as she reached up and put her hand on his jaw. "Condom?"

"Locked and ready," Spencer said with a grin. As Noreen laughed, he slowly entered. They both froze and stared at each other at the feel of him inside her. "You're so tight."

"You're so big." They exchanged grins, but Noreen lost all train of thought when Spencer began to move.

"Look at me," Spencer said between clenched teeth and sighed in relief when she opened her eyes. "That's better." He moved, and when he felt her inner walls tighten, he reached between them and played with her clit. When she started to become undone, he bent down and kissed her, absorbing her scream. As he felt her cum, it caused Spencer to release his own orgasm. When he felt he could move, he moved to the side and brought her with him.

"I'm sorry," he said after regaining his breath.

"What for? That was wonderful."

"I thought I could last longer than I did."

"You got me off. That's the only thing that matters." She raised herself up on her elbow, then stared down at him.

"What?"

"Maybe you need more practice so you can last longer next time."

Spencer stared at her in shock, then roared with laughter. "Yeah, maybe you're right." He rolled over and kissed her. It was several hours and several orgasms later when they called it a halt for the night.

"Stay," Noreen said sleepily when she felt the bed move as Spencer sat up on the edge of it.

"Are you sure?"

"I am."

"Okay," Spencer said as he rose to use the facilities, then came back and crawled beneath the blankets with her. As he settled her against him, he ran his hand up and down her back. "This is a first for me."

"What?" Noreen asked in sleepy confusion. "Sex?"

"No, spending the night."

"Oh." Nothing more was said, and after some time, Spencer looked down and smiled when he saw the woman in his arms was sound asleep. It didn't take long for him to follow.

CHAPTER 13

SPENCER LOOKED up from his desk at the heavy pounding on his office door and scowled at the man standing there.

"You need to come to the front office," Logan bit out. He turned on his heel but barked over his shoulder, "Now."

Surprised by Logan's tone and attitude, though it wasn't anything new, Spencer followed him. "What's going on?" he asked as he caught up with the other man.

"A fucking mess, and it's all because of you." Logan didn't say anything after that, and Spencer felt like he was somehow being set up. As he approached, he saw his buddies in the hall looking frazzled.

"What's going on?"

"I know we helped you fill out those flyers for your talk at the school," Nash began. "I don't think any of us thought you would get more than a few people inquiring about your class."

"Yeah, that's what we discussed. What's the problem?"

"There are over a hundred people here asking for information about your class. We had to take them to the main conference room." They looked up when the door opened, and another group of kids and parents walked in. "See what I mean?" Logan spoke then.

"Okay, let me get over there." Spencer paused long enough to look at the others. "Do you want to see if you can get more clients? Maybe we can give them a deal if they sign up for more than one program." He waited for three minutes as the others seemed to think about his proposal and sighed in relief when they nodded. Together, the five of them headed in the direction of the conference room.

"I'll stay back and direct anyone else that comes in," Logan said. "Did you tell these people to be here at this time?"

"No, but since school is out this week, maybe they thought they could get here bright and early to sign up."

"Do you have a schedule ready?" Nash asked him as they walked down the hall.

"No, I'll just give my speech, then I'll give them an application. If they get upset, I'll just tell them the flyer I passed out at school was informational."

"That'll work," Simon said as he broke off and joined them just before they entered the room. He held a flyer and grinned at Spencer's confused look. "Applications, I was updating them last week." Spencer nodded and opened the door. They heard a lot of talking from the outside, but the second he walked through the door, the occupants quieted down.

"Welcome," Spencer said as he stood tall before the people standing there. "I'm assuming you're all here because of the flyers I passed out at the school last week?" When the others said they were, he continued. "I know what I'm about to say will disappoint all of you, but it has to be this way. The flyer I passed out was an informational one. You'll have to fill out an application, and when I get them back, I can start scheduling classes. Though all of you will be able to take a class, unfortunately, you can't take one at the same time."

"What he means," Darius said as he stepped forward. "Will the cabin he trains in safely hold thirty students at a time? There's a spot on the application if you would like to take a class with a certain individual, then please fill it out. We can't start any classes today with you, and I'm sorry if you had hoped to do that. However, as I'm sure you all know, we need to get the paperwork out of the way first, then we'll have to schedule you for classes."

"When are the classes held?" Someone in the crowd asked.

"I'm already booked on Mondays and Fridays I will schedule you guys on Tuesdays, Thursdays, and Saturdays. The Tuesday and Thursday classes will run for an hour starting at five at night. All my classes last for an hour. Saturdays will start at nine, and I can have three that day. On the application, please specify what day you would like."

"What if we want to take classes?" A woman in the crowd had raised her hand to ask. "Can we take classes at a different time than our children?"

"You may, as I said, state the day you want on the application. I'll be honest here, I hadn't expected this many of you to come forward. It will take a few days to go through the applications, and to get organized."

"What about the Martial Arts that you teach?" One of the boys Spencer had talked to after the presentation on Friday asked. "What if I want to take Karate?"

"Then that would be a totally different application, and there are other fees involved than just the self-defense class."

"What fees?" The same boy asked.

"You'll have to pay for you Gi, which is the white uniform you wear. You will be responsible for either paying me to purchase one for you, or purchase one for yourself. I can give you a list of websites to order from. I, on the other hand, will be responsible for passing out the colored belts you earn." He looked at the crowd, then nodded. "This first application we'll be handing out is for the self-defense classes." Spencer paused when he looked up and Logan entered carrying a box, with several people trailing behind him.

"More recruits," he said as he set the box on the floor beside Spencer. "I took the liberty of printing up the copies of your fees and services. I even put them in folders." He looked at the other man with a scowl. "You owe me."

Spencer smirked then nodded his thanks. For the next hour, paperwork was passed around, and Spencer answered questions along with the other four men. By the time they all left, Spencer was exhausted. He looked at the stack of papers on the table and shook his head.

"What did I do?"

The others laughed at him. "Opened Pandora's box. But, look on the bright side. If you can get through to these kids, maybe they'll have a better chance on the outside world. If bullying is as problematic as you say it is in the school, then maybe they can help prevent a major catastrophe from happening. Not only for standing up for themselves, but also for doing their little part of keeping the peace around them." Nash nodded as he picked up a stack of papers that was at least three inches thick.

"Are you helping me with the applications?" Spencer asked hopefully.

"No, these are applications for my Yoga classes."

"Wow."

"Yeah, and I thought I had my paperwork done for the week." Nash shook his head as he left the conference room. Spencer looked at the stacks of papers, and instead of going to his office, he went to the break room to fix himself a cup of coffee, then went back to the conference room. He picked up the first application, and started to make piles. By the time he was finished with all the applications, it was time to get changed to go to his Monday night self-defense class, to be quickly followed by a Martial Arts class.

NOREEN FELT on top of the world. It wasn't because she ended up staying three hours after her regular shift to help the new girl close up. And it wasn't because she had been running since she entered the diner thirty minutes before her shift. It also wasn't because of all the money she'd been able to pocket. No, she contributed her good mood to the fact that she'd had sex for the first time in years last night, and it was the best she'd ever had. Not that she had much to compare it to. Chloe's father was the only one she'd ever been with. No, she contributed her good mood to Spencer. He had still been there when the alarm had gone off, and after having some hot shower sex, he had left for the day, asking if he could return that night. However, he couldn't be there until ten. He had classes until nine, then he had to clean up afterward. Noreen had readily agreed for him to come over. With a smile on her face, she got into her SUV and headed for home.

Ten minutes from her home, she frowned when she saw headlights in the distance behind her, but they were coming fast. At one point, she glanced in the rearview mirror and swore when she was blinded when the lights behind her suddenly became blinding. The next thing she knew, both her and her vehicle were shot forward when the other one hit her from behind.

"Don't panic," Noreen repeated the mantra several times. Several things went through her mind at once. *Single female, alone, at night, in the dark. She had to get to Chloe. She wanted to call Spencer. Where were the cops when you needed one?* These thoughts went through her head as she fought to keep control of her vehicle. As she rounded a bend, she thought she had a reprieve when she saw another car coming toward her. But if she thought the person hitting her from behind would back off, she was sadly mistaken. Suddenly, she was hit so hard she could barely control the vehicle. The asshat from behind didn't let up and Noreen ended up being pushed into the path of the oncoming car. The last thing she heard was her screaming, and the blare of horns before she blacked out.

"Miss? Miss? Are you okay?" Noreen heard a distant voice and moaned as she came too. "Don't move, help is on the way," the voice said. Noreen could only moan harder. Her entire body hurt and she didn't want to open her eyes, let alone try to get out of the vehicle. She heard sirens in the distance, but didn't move to try to help herself. She must have blacked out again because the next thing she knew, someone was calling her by name.

"Noreen? Noreen, are you with us?"

Noreen moaned and tried to open her eyes. "I'm awake."

"Thank god," came the male voice and Noreen pried open her eyes to look at the person who had said that with such anguish.

"Spencer? What are you doing here?"

"I was coming to your place and caught the tail end of your accident."

"It wasn't an accident."

"I know, I saw someone push you toward the oncoming traffic. The police and ambulance are on the way."

"Chloe, I have to tell Chloe," Noreen said as she struggled to get out of the vehicle. She didn't have the strength to do more than glower when Spencer held her back.

"I'll go tell Chloe and bring her to wherever you end up. But not until I make sure you're okay. The ambulance just pulled up. I'll stay with you until they can get down here to you."

"What do you mean? Down here to me?"

"Sweetie, the asshat who run you off the road pushed you into a ravine. You're about twenty to thirty feet down. I don't want to scare you, but if there hadn't been anyone around to witness what happened, no one would be able to find you for hours, or maybe even days."

"Shit," Noreen said and reached for his hand. "Thank you."

"No problem. The EMTs are here now, I'm going to go up and talk to the sheriff."

"Thank you," Noreen said and hadn't realized she was crying until he reached in and gently wiped her tears with his thumb. Before he left her, he leaned in and kissed her gently on the lips. He didn't bother wiping the blood away before he did so. When the EMTs arrived and asked him questions, he answered to the best of his ability, then listened as they started talking to Noreen. When he heard she was lucid enough to answer them, he climbed the hill, pulling out his phone on the way, and sent a group text. At the top of the hill, he sighed in relief when he saw the police officer on the scene was Sparrow. He waited to the side of the road until she made her way over to him. He told her exactly what he had seen, and why he had gone down to the wreck.

They stood off to the side to talk, then they watched as the fire department arrived and went down to help with extracting Noreen from her vehicle. When the jaws of life came into play, Spencer winced, but made a quick decision.

"Sparrow, I need you to do me a favor."

"What's that?"

"I need you to call you husband here to the scene. Have him bring Swede with him."

"Why would I want to do that?"

"Because there's something I didn't tell you, and I want to tell you, but not until I see Stone and Swede, along with my guys from The Centre." As he spoke a vehicle pulled up to the scene and Darius, Simon, Nash, and Logan got out.

"What's going on?" Logan was the first to reach them.

"Someone ran Noreen off the road." He pointed down the hill, then looked directly at Sparrow as he said the next part. "I have a plate number, and I think I know who it is. But I was Stone and Swede here first."

"You won't leave me out of any of this?"

"I won't, I promise," he said as he held up his hand and when she walked away, he turned to the others. "I caught a glimpse of the driver that pushed Noreen into the line of traffic. I am about ninety percent sure it is the guy who is after us."

"Fuck," Logan said while the others answered his sentiment. They stood there and watched the scene below while they waited for the two men to arrive.

CHAPTER 14

SPENCER WALKED over to the gurney as soon as it reached the top of the hill. He winced when he saw all the dried, and still oozing blood on her head and face. He didn't let that stop him from leaning down and kissing her forehead. "I'll go get Chloe and bring her to the hospital. I have some more questions to answer first, but I'll be right behind you."

"Thank you, I hate to ask this of you, but could you have Chloe get some clothes for me? I don't think these will last."

"I will, anything in particular?"

"Yes, tell her to pack my binge-watching clothes. She'll know what I'm talking about. They are in the bottom of my white dresser." That was the last thing she said before she passed out again.

"We'll have to check her out at the hospital," Seth Falco came up to him then. "My diagnosis is a severe concussion. They may keep her overnight for observation."

"Thanks for the heads up, Seth. I'll let Chloe know when I go pick her up." They shook hands, and as they people began cleaning up the scene and hooking up a wrecker to Noreen's vehicle, Spencer walked over to the growing crowd around the police cruiser.

"What's up?" Stone asked as he stood next to his wife.

Spencer turned to Sparrow and nodded once. "I'm sorry, but I withheld information from you. I know you're the law, but these guys helped us out in the past. It's that past information they dug up that comes into play here."

"How so?" Swede and Sparrow asked as one.

"I witnessed the tail end of Noreen's accident. I saw someone shove a vehicle into the line of oncoming traffic. The driver coming toward us was able to avoid the collision, but Noreen was pushed over the edge. I was close enough to get a look at the guy, and I have his plate number."

"Okay, but how does that involve us? Sparrow should be able to help you."

Spencer pulled out his phone, accessed something, then turned it to show them the still in the video. "This is the guy you told us the fuckwad hired to take us out."

"Shit," both Swede and Stone said. Stone turned to

his wife to explain. Minutes later, Sparrow asked with raised brow.

"You saw this guy behind the wheel of the vehicle that hit Noreen's?"

"I did, and this is the plate number." Spencer reached into his pocket and pulled out a rumpled napkin. The only thing he had to write on when he watched as Noreen went over the edge. "I didn't know it was Noreen until I got down there. I got the plate number, checked on the other vehicle, then made my way down there. Sparrow, I know this might not mean anything, but then again, it might mean everything. I started dating Noreen. The first attack against her was when two of her tires were slashed over at Gunny's last week. Now this. The photo I showed you is from the video I took the day you came in and helped Faulkner when Mattie fired Jennifer."

She stood there with her hands on her hips, and looked off into the distance. Spencer looked at Stone, and he only smiled and shook his head as he taped the side of his forehead, indicating that the women was thinking. She looked at them finally and shook her head.

"Okay, thank you for being honest with me. I'm assuming you asked me to have Stone and Swede here so you can ask them to look into the matter?"

"Correct."

"I'll allow it, but I will also be looking into it." She

turned to the two men from the Brotherhood Protection Agency. "I want copies of the reports you dig up."

"Agreed," they both said and nodded to her.

"Good, I'm going to finish up here, then drive over to see if I can't get a statement from Noreen. Will you be there?" She asked Spencer.

"I have to go get Chloe."

"Who's that?" Nash scowled at him. "I thought you said you were dating Noreen."

"I am. Chloe is her fourteen-year-old daughter that is home alone."

"Ah," they all said, and Spencer left to head to Noreen's house. At the front door, he found himself suddenly nervous as he knocked. It was opened several minutes later by Chloe.

"Hey, Mom's not home from work yet. She had to work late."

"Can I come in?"

"I shouldn't let you, because I'm here alone."

"I know, but Chloe, I really need to talk to you." There must have been something in his expression or his tone that alerted her. She stepped back and he saw her knuckles turn white as she held onto the doorknob.

"There's been an accident."

"Is she dead?"

"No!" Spencer quickly reassured her and caught her

as her knees buckled. With her cradled in his arms, he shut the door with his foot, and carried the young girl to the living room. He sat on the couch and held her as she cried. "She's going to be okay, but they took her to the hospital to check her out. When I saw her, she was talking, but they had to transport her in the ambulance. I was a few miles behind her, and saw part of what happened. I don't want to alarm you, and I have to talk to your mother about this, but I believe someone is after me and is using your mother to get to me."

"But how did they even know you were dating, you only just started."

"I know, and I have my suspicions, I'm having some people I know, as well as the police looking into it. If what I suspect is true, then you also may be in danger. I can't let that happen."

"Does Mom know any of this?"

"No, I was going to tell her about it when we got to know each other better."

"Sleeping together on your first date isn't getting to know each other better?" Chloe asked with a smirk as she rose to her feet and scrubbed the tears from her face. She laughed heartily at his shocked expression. "Did you at least use a condom?"

"I did," Spencer automatically answered, then chuckled when she winked at him.

"So, why are you really here?"

"To tell you about you mother's accident, and to

take you to the hospital to see her. If you would like to go."

"Yes, let me change."

"Wait," Spencer called as Chloe ran toward the stairs. "Noreen said she wanted her binge-watching clothes in the bottom of her white dresser."

"Got it," Chloe said and ran up the stairs. She came back seconds later. "There's leftover lasagna in the refrigerator if you want to heat some up to eat before we go."

Spencer was about to refuse until his stomach rumbled, and he made his way to the kitchen. By the time he was done, he had finished a hearty helping and was waiting for Chloe by the door.

"Do you have your keys?" Spencer asked as he opened the door for them and nodded when Chloe held up a ring of them. They were silent as they went out to his truck, after he helped her inside, he went around and got behind the wheel. They stayed silent until they were closer to the hospital Seth had told Spencer they were taking her.

"How bad is she?"

"I don't know. I'm not saying that to placate you, I'm saying it because I genuinely don't know. I do know she had a cut on her head and one on her cheekbone, but I don't know the extent of those injuries. She was out of it when I got to her, and she passed out a couple of times. Don't quote me, but I'm thinking she might have a severe concussion and may have to spend the night in the hospital."

"Okay, and I don't want to sound needy, but what about me?"

"What about you?"

"I know I'm of legal age to stay by myself, but if Mom's in the hospital for a night or even two, what do I do?"

"Would you be okay if I stay at the house with you? Make sure you're safe, and that nobody tries to get you. I can sleep on the couch."

"That couch is horrible," Chloe laughed. "I would feel safer if you were there, the only other question is can I go to work with you? I don't want to stay home by myself. I'll be there for Mom when she gets out of the hospital, but I don't want to be there all day all alone."

"I don't have a problem with it. I'm sure if you don't have a book to read, or something to do we can find you something."

"Thank you." Chloe seemed to relax after that and they finished the drive in silence.

"What are you thinking now?" Spencer asked as he helped her from the truck and saw her pensive expression.

"If Mom is really hurt and has to be in the hospital for a day or two, someone should tell Mattie."

"I'll mention that to Sparrow," Spencer said as he

walked beside her and pointed to the police cruiser that just pulled into the lot. They waited for her to catch up, then together the three of the strode into the doors of the emergency room. Spencer wanted to take over, but he let Sparrow do it. He figured the badge and uniform would get quicker results than him trying to throw his weight around. They didn't have time to wait, and when the nurse on duty asked who he and Chloe were, Sparrow didn't miss a beat and said they were Noreen's husband and child.

Sparrow turned to them with a shrug, "Sorry, it was easier than trying to explain."

"With you saying that, does that mean I can go in and see Mom?"

"Yes, but you'll probably have to have Spencer here as an escort. Being an adult and all."

"Thank you," Chloe said and her next action surprised both Spencer and Sparrow as she hugged the deputy. She stepped back and wiped her eyes. "I've never had to do something like this. I've never even visited anyone in the hospital before."

"Stick with Spencer, I'm sure he knows his way around a hospital."

"I do." Spencer admitted and they all looked up when a doctor approached them.

"Rafferty?"

"Us," Spencer said and wrapped his arm around a suddenly shaking Chloe. "How is Noreen?"

"Roughed up, but with a few days rest she will recover nicely."

Spencer was grateful for the arm around Chloe. It afforded him the opportunity to catch her when her knees buckled. "How bad is Mom roughed up?"

"Cuts, bruises, nothing major except for a concussion. We'll be keeping her overnight for observation. But she received no broken bones, no internal injuries, and no brain trauma."

"Thank god," Spencer whispered, and Chloe whipped her head around and stared at him in shock. "It's a good thing, Chloe." He hugged her to reassure her and was suddenly hit with a wave of paternal love when she wrapped her arms around him and laid her head on his chest. As he continued to hold her, he felt her shaking begin to subside.

"I'll go talk to her first," Sparrow said, and Spencer gave her a nod over Chloe's head. He didn't want Chloe to hear the nasty details until he was ready to tell both of them why he thinks Noreen had been targeted. If he wanted any type of relationship with the two of them, he had better come clean as soon as Noreen was released from the hospital. If she kicks him out of her life for the potential harm he brought to her and her daughter, he would understand. But that wouldn't prevent him from still keeping them safe from harm.

Sparrow returned an hour later and only gave Spencer a nod. "I got everything I need. Visiting hours are over, but I convinced the nurse to let the two of you go back to see her. They'll be moving her upstairs to a bed afterward. She's groggy, but wants to see both of you." Sparrow reached into her pocket and pulled out a card to hand to Chloe. "Since you're under age, stick with Spencer while you're here. Here's my card, if you need anything you don't hesitate to call. My personal cell number is on the back." She nodded as Chloe took the card, then turned to leave.

"I'm scared," Chloe whispered as they stood outside the curtain her mother was behind.

"I know you are, and I'm here for you. I don't know how you are about blood, but I do know of a couple of cuts she had on her face. I'm sure you know that head wounds bleed more than regular wounds."

"I do, and it's Mom who's a ninny when it comes to blood. She doesn't pass out, but she gets queasy in the stomach, and she sort of weaves back and forth. I've learned to clean up my own cuts to spare her the hassle."

Spencer grinned at her. "Hopefully, the only time she'll see the cuts is when she looks in a mirror." They shared and smile, then Chloe gripped his hand as he reached up to open the curtain. "You've got this," he whispered as he slid the material to the side.

CHAPTER 15

SPENCER STARED at the woman lying in the bed and it took everything he had not to rush to her side, pick her up, and cradle her in his arms. She looked so small and defenseless. He didn't know which was whiter, the bedding beneath her, or her face.

"Mom?" Chloe asked quietly, and rushed forward when Noreen gingerly turned her head to look at her daughter. When she held her hand out to her, Chloe dropped Spencer's and rushed forward. He followed, standing right behind the younger woman.

"Spencer," Noreen said as she reached up and took his hand in hers. "Thank you for bringing Chloe to me."

"I can't say long, Mom," Chloe said. "You have to stay in the hospital, and we talked, but I invited Spencer to sleep in our house."

"Are you okay with that?" Noreen frowned at

Spencer, who winced when he saw the tape over her stitches pull. He automatically reached up and rubbed his thumb gently over the frown lines.

"I am. Chloe can even come to work with me tomorrow." When it looked like she was about to protest, he shook his head at her. "I've got this. Chloe and I will be a team, you just need to get better. We'll be here tomorrow after work, I can get away at any time, call me if you are released before lunch."

"I don't know where my purse and phone are," Noreen said, and tried to scowl, but Chloe gripped her hand.

"We'll find them. Maybe Sparrow has them with your truck."

"Maybe." Noreen sighed. A nurse walked in and said they were ready to take her to a room upstairs, and after Chloe hugged her mother and told her to rest, that all would be good, she stepped out, and Noreen stopped Spencer from leaving.

"Does she know how it happened?"

"No, I only told her you had been in an accident. I figured you could tell her yourself when you get home."

"Thank you."

"You're welcome. Don't worry about Chloe. Though I've never been around teenagers, I got this. Your job is to get better, and come home tomorrow. I'll leave my contact information with the nurse and have them contact me if you can come home earlier than when I get out of work at five."

"Okay," Noreen said sleepily, then smiled as Spencer leaned down and kissed her forehead.

"We need to talk when you're on the mend. I think I know why you were targeted. It's not a conversation to have now, and I'm sorry I brought it up, but it has to be said. If you don't want anything to do with me after I explain it all, then I understand."

"Are you married and have kids?"

"No, why would you even ask that?" Spencer reared back in utter confusion at her statement.

"Other than you being married, having kids, or in a serious relationship with someone else, and you're just playing the field with me, there's nothing that would stop me from continuing to see you."

"Oh." Spencer didn't know what else to say, so he kissed her forehead again, then stepped back as the nurses got her IVs transferred to the other bed, and they moved her from one to the other. Spencer winced right along with Noreen when they jostled her around. In the hall, the nurse stopped long enough for Chloe to say goodbye to her mother and that she would see her the next day. They stood in the empty hall for several minutes before Spencer walked over and put his arm around her shoulder.

"You okay?"

"Thank you for bringing me. I think I would have freaked out all night not knowing what was wrong with her. She's going to continue to bruise for a few days, but I feel better that I was able to see her." She hugged him, then looked at him tiredly. "I'm ready to go home."

"Then let's go." Spencer walked down the hall with his arm wrapped around hers, and they only stopped long enough to get the nurse to put his contact information in Noreen's file. Both were silent on the ride home. Just before they entered town, Chloe turned to him.

"Do you need to go to your place to get some clothes?"

"Sure," Spencer said as he turned right instead of turning left, and three blocks down the road, he pulled up to the curb. "You're welcome to come in. I shouldn't be more than a few minutes."

Chloe hopped out of the truck and grinned at him when he laughed. "It's not much," he said as he inserted his key in the lock, and led them into an apartment. "I'll be right back," he said as he turned on lights and headed toward the back of the space. While he was gone, Chloe looked around, then ended up walking the outside walls. Spencer found her in the middle of an empty room halfway down the hall. "You okay?"

"I'm fine, but I've never seen a place so empty, as well as so clean. I swear you could eat off your kitchen floor, it's so shiny."

Spencer laughed as he swung his duffle over his

shoulder and pointed to the front door. "Decades of being in the military. Everything in its place, everything has its place."

"But does that make you a minimalist?"

"No," Spencer laughed as he locked up after them. On the way back to the truck he explained. "Being in the military for so long, I lived on bases all over the world. I was assigned a certain amount of space, and it had to be cleaned per military regulations. The last time I ever had any room to myself was before I enlisted at the age of eighteen. I'm forty-two, or will be on my next birthday. I left my parent's home to join the military, and only got out a little over a year ago."

"Ah, so you haven't had time to collect any sort of junk yet."

"Correct," Spencer laughed as he helped her into the truck and went around to the driver's side. When they arrived at Noreen's place, Chloe reached for the door handle and sighed when Spencer gave her a glowering look. She removed her hand and sat back until he got out and came over to open the door for her. When they arrived at the front door, he took her keys from her, and told her to stay outside. He returned less than five minutes later to tell her she could come in.

"Is that a gun?" Chloe asked in shock as she looked down at his thigh and saw he held a gun in his hand. It quickly disappeared behind his back.

"Yes, just making sure there's no one inside." He let her in, and looked around the space as they both removed their shoes. "You need an alarm."

"You'll have to talk to Mom about it," Chloe said tiredly. "I'm wiped out, what time do we have to leave for your work tomorrow?"

"Seven."

"I'll see you then," Chloe said and shocked Spencer when she came over to him and stood on her toes to kiss his cheek. As she stepped away, she looked him directly in the eye. "Thank you for taking me to see Mom. I don't know what I would have done if you hadn't been there."

Spencer was too shocked to reply, and by the time he thought of what to say, she was already halfway up the stairs. Instead of going directly to bed, he raided the refrigerator again and had another piece of lasagna. After he cleaned up the entire kitchen, he walked the house to check that the doors and windows were locked and secure. He made a mental note to talk to Noreen about getting an alarm installed. The first thing he would have to do is find out if she owned or rented, he could take it from there. An hour later he settled in Noreen's bed and held her pillow to him. He knew it was sappy, but the smell of her on her pillow eased him into a deep slumber.

～

THE NEXT MORNING, Spencer had been up and raided the kitchen. He found the makings for French Toast, and added some bacon with it. By the time Chloe joined him, he had it almost cooked and felt pride that she immediately sat down and began eating. They were only a few minutes past his allotted time for when they had to leave, but he felt good that he had been successful in giving her a hearty breakfast. When they arrived at The Centre, Spencer looked at Chloe with a raised brow when he saw her reach for the door handle, and grinned when she dropped her hand, and blew out her breath hard enough to ruffle her bangs. He got out and came around the open the door for her. They walked side by side as they entered the front entrance of the building. Spencer didn't know if he should be shocked or not that all his friends were there. He didn't hesitate to make the introductions.

"Hey, this is Chloe. She's Noreen's daughter. Noreen had a concussion and was kept overnight for observation. Nothing was broken, nor did she sustain any internal injuries, and her brain scan came back clean. Doctor said she had a lot of bruises as well as cuts and scrapes. She should be released sometime today." Once he received nods from the others, he turned to Chloe.

"Chloe, these are the guys I work with. They are also the ones I did military service with."

"The ones that someone bullied you out of your careers?"

"Correct." Spencer nodded and turned to point. "Darius, Simon, Nash, and Logan. While I do the self-defense and Martial Arts training, these guys do other things."

"We'll get into that later," Logan said after he shook Chloe's hand. "Sorry to be gruff, but we have a meeting to get to. You can't come."

"That's okay," Chloe wasn't taken aback by his gruffness. "Give me a chair and I'll be out of your hair."

"Let me take you to my office," Spencer said and led her down the hall. He opened the door and after Chloe looked around, she headed to a comfortable looking chair in the corner. She turned to him with a smirk. "What?"

"Your office is furnished better than your apartment."

Spencer laughed, shook his head, and told her where the break room was if she wanted to get something to drink. When he was reassured she had everything, he turned on his heel and went to the conference room. He filled a coffee cup on the way. As he entered, it shocked him to realize that three men from the Brotherhood Protection Agency was there. He nodded to Swede, Stone, and Jake. Before he was even settled they demanded to know who Noreen was, and he updated them.

"What brings you here?"

"On the way home from the accident scene last night, I called Jake and told him what was up," Swede began. "Because I had done a background check on the shooter that was after Simon and Jocelyn, I still had the file I had worked up on the guy. His name is Nate Renaldo, and he is here on a VISA."

"What nationality is he?" Nash asked calmly.

"Syrian. After a lot of digging, it turns out that he has ties to a well-known Syrian Insurgent group."

Spencer looked at his buddies and scowled. "How much do you want to bet The Fuckwad is behind all this?"

"If you're talking about Wally Mathias, then my bet is ninety-nine-point nine percent accurate," Jake spoke for the first time. "After my guys ran their reports, the gave me the findings, and I called them into Patterson."

"Why?" Spencer asked. "What can he do about the results of your investigation?"

"Stone?" Jake said and looked over at the other man.

"I ran the plate you gave Sparrow. It turns out it came back to a corporation that sponsored Renaldo's VISA. It's a dummy corporation. It took several hours of digging, but both you and Jake are correct. Wally Mathias owns that corporation."

"With further digging," Swede spoke again. "Nothing is concrete yet, but that's why we called

Hank, he has more power than we do to get some information. Gentlemen, it looks like this Mathias character hired Renaldo to take you out. Hank's preliminary findings date back to it happening while you were still active-duty military."

The five former JSOC members looked at one another, and as one, they jumped to their feet and began swearing and talking at once. The guys from the Brotherhood remained silent. Finally, after at least ten minutes of ranting and raving, Spencer turned to the others.

"How much do I owe you for the information?"

"On the house," Jake said as he pushed a file toward Spencer. "It's all in there. Keep it safe."

"Thanks," Spencer said as he shook their hands, then turned to Jake with a frown. "Do you guys put in security systems?"

"We can, who are we talking about?"

"Noreen and her daughter. Chloe's in my office as we speak, but I would feel better if they had a security system."

"Let me write something up for you and get back to you."

"Thanks." Spencer watched as the men left then turned to the others to see they were still in shock. "Hopefully Patterson can speak with who he has to and get this information to the powers that be about reinstating our military status." He looked at Darius with a frown. "Can we take this to Fenmore?"

"We could, but I don't think it would do any good."

"Why not?" Nash asked.

"She was kicked off the case when the two of us hooked up. If she comes forward then it would look like she's not being partial because of our relationship. No, I trust Patterson to get the information in the right hands." There was nothing else Spencer could say, so he grabbed the file Jake gave him and headed back to his office. He stopped by to refill his coffee mug and grabbed a bottle of juice from the refrigerator. He walked into his office and stood there in shock.

"Stop!" Chloe called out as Spencer started to enter. He froze and looked around.

"What the hell is all this?"

"Don't be mad at me, but I was bored. I looked at the piles of stuff on you desk. Yes, I was being nosy, and I'm sorry if it upsets you, but I saw your notes first of how to get all these people signed up for classes." She drew in a deep breath and let it out in a rush, then downed half the bottle of juice he handed her. He wasn't mad at her, he just wanted to know what she was doing. Her expression showed excitement, so he let her talk.

"I wrote down what you had on the whiteboard, then I erased it. I started making a chart of the times you're available, then a list of the people who signed up. I know most of them, since I go to school with them. There are some things on the applications some of them forgot to mention."

"Like?" Spencer asked as he gingerly walked through the piles of papers on the floor to reach her standing before the whiteboard.

"Like this person is in Math club after school on Tuesday's."

Spencer nodded and listened to her explain what she had done, and they spent the next couple of hours working on it. At the end, he was happy with what they had come up with, and told her so.

"Let's go see your mother. I'll buy you lunch on the way."

"Can we get it on the way back? Maybe Mom can come home and we can all get something to eat, together."

"I like that idea."

Spencer went to tell the others what he would be doing, and they said it was okay if he took the rest of the day off, just be back for his classes that started later in the afternoon.

CHAPTER 16

"Why do you do that?" Chloe asked in frustration when Spencer opened the vehicle door for her to climb in before he got behind the wheel. "I can open my own door, you know."

"I know, it's just something my father instilled into me at an early age. He told me a gentleman always opened a door for a lady. If you find the right boy, they'll open the door for you, and even pull your chair out for you at a restaurant. It's a good manners thing to do."

Chloe snorted a laugh, causing Spencer to look at her with a frown. "All the boys I know would probably pull my chair out just to see me land on my ass." She giggled then looked at him with wide eyes. "Don't tell Mom I swore."

Spencer couldn't help it, he laughed. They shared a comfortable silence on the way to the hospital, and didn't say anything until they stood outside the room they had been direct to. Spencer looked down at Chloe when she gripped his hand hard as he reached up to open the door that had been left slightly ajar.

"I'm scared."

"I know, I've got you." He squeezed her hand and opened the door, bracing himself for what he was about to walk in and see. Seeing Noreen sitting up on the side of the bed and dressed in the clothes Chloe had brought her the night before eased some of his anxiety.

"Mom," Chloe said as she dropped Spencer's hand and rushed to her mother. Spencer noted as she moved her head quickly, she turned white, and her knuckled tightened on the sheets beside her, but that didn't prevent her from hugging her daughter.

"Chloe," Noreen breathed out a sigh of relief. "How are you?"

"I'm fine, the question is, how are you?"

"Sore, extremely sore, and there's a bongo playing in my head."

"Is that something we should be worried about?"

"No, the doctor said I would probably have a headache for a few days. He told me to only be worried if it gets worse than it is right now." She looked over at Spencer and gave him a sweet smile. The bruises on her face ruined it, but he took what she gave him.

"Hey," Noreen said softly to him.

Spencer knew it wasn't the time, but her voice went right to his cock. He gave himself a mental slap, and hurried forward. Instead of hugging her, he bent down and kissed not only her forehead, but also her cheek. Right near where there were several butterfly bandages.

"Thank you for taking care of my little girl."

"She's not little, but you're welcome. It was a pleasure."

"Mom," Chloe said with a giggle. "I had to remind Spencer to pick up some clothes for himself and I saw his apartment."

"Okay," Noreen said, trying not to be jealous, then she frowned as she picked up on her daughter's excitement. "Was there something special about it?"

"He doesn't have anything," she laughed. "I mean there's one chair in the living room, and the two rooms I assumed were spare bedrooms were completely empty. I didn't see his bedroom, because that's just gross, but we have more stuff in our attic than he does in his entire apartment." Chloe grinned as she looked over at Spencer. "Our attic is almost empty."

Spencer laughed and help Noreen stand when she tried to on her own. He wrapped his arms around her and liked that she held onto his belt loops. She looked at him with a smile. "I'll have to come check it out sometime."

"You will," he said as he bent and kissed her forehead. They both looked up when the door opened and a nurse walked in, followed by Sparrow, dressed in her work uniform.

"Let me go over the doctor's instructions with your family," the nurse said and Chloe stood there to listen and ask any questions. When she was done, she smiled at Noreen, still wrapped in Spencer's arms. "I'll go order a wheelchair for you, then you're free to go. If your headache gets any worse, call your doctor immediately."

"I will, thank you," Noreen said and turned to Sparrow.

"I see you're on the mend," Sparrow said as she lifted a bag and placed it on the bed. "I had your SUV towed to the police yard. It's going to be a couple of days before forensics are done with it, but you should be able to contact your insurance carrier. Here's a folder with the police report, and anything your insurance company may need." She placed the file on the bed beside the bag. "The bag contains your purse and phone. I went though the purse for you insurance information, and saw your phone inside. Can't say if the batter is dead or not, but at least you have it."

"Thank you."

"You're welcome, and Spencer, Stone dropped this off to me to give to you when he found out I was coming here." She walked over and handed him another file and watched as Spencer flipped it open, then back closed. "Thank you." He looked at Noreen and Chloe. "It's quotes to get you a security system. Do you own or rent?"

"Own. Does that make a difference?"

"We'll talk about it, but yes, this means you can put in what you want, or can afford, verses what the landlord thinks you should have."

Noreen slowly nodded and thanked Sparrow. As soon as the deputy left, someone arrived with a wheelchair. Spencer and Chloe exchanged looks when Noreen sank into it.

"Sorry, but just that little bit of walking, standing, and talked exhausted me. I'll gladly take a ride to the front door."

They walked beside her and when they reached the main floor, Spencer sped up and said he would go get his truck. By the time Noreen had been wheeled outside, he was there waiting for her. He had the two passenger doors open and grinned when Chloe climbed into the back, holding her mother's possessions. Spencer made sure he had a tight grip on her arm to steady her as she stood from the wheelchair, then he let her set the pace to get to the truck. At the door, he looked at her with a cocked brow.

"May I?"

"What?" Noreen asked in confusion, then gave a squeak when he picked her up and placed her in the front seat. He even leaned in and snapped her buckle in place. After he shut the door, he climbed inside and heard Chloe tell her mother that she better get used to Spencer opening the door for her, because he had done that with her for the past two days. Spencer only threw a look at her, along with a grin.

"A gentleman," Noreen sighed as she placed her hand over his forearm as they drove. He didn't even make it out of the parking lot before he looked over at her. "Chloe and I were going to get some lunch before we came to see you, but she convinced me to wait until you were out. Would you like something to eat?"

"I would, I know I shouldn't, but I would like to stop into the diner and talk with Mattie. The doctor gave me orders to be out of work for the rest of the week. I want to explain to her what happened. If we could order, I could talk to her as it's being made, then, if you agree, I'd like to take it home to eat."

"That can be arranged. Do you know what you want? Chloe and I can order as you go talk with Mattie."

"My usual," Noreen said and closed her eyes. Spencer looked at Chloe in confusion. The girl giggled.

"BLT on sourdough, extra T, lightly toasted. Sweet fries, and absolutely, positively no pickles."

"You got it," Noreen said with her eyes still closed.

"I got all that, except for the sweet fries. What are they?"

"Sweet potato French fries."

"Ah, got it." He put the truck in gear and headed back to town. When they were on main street, Noreen roused long enough to give Spencer directions so they could park in the back of the restaurant and she could go in that way. As soon as they parked, Spencer jumped out, but not before throwing a look at Chloe. Once he opened her door, he whispered to her to go inside and get Mattie, then place their order. He pulled is wallet and told her what he wanted, before he handed her some cash.

"You're staying there," Spencer told Noreen. "Chloe will bring Mattie out." Less than five minutes later, the woman in question came hurrying around the front of the truck. She took one look at Noreen and cried out like she was in pain.

"Noreen! Oh my god, how are you? Sparrow called me last night and said you had been in an accident. Is it because I've been working you so hard? I'll step up my game and hire someone, I promise."

"It's not that," Noreen said and looked at Spencer. "I don't know what to say."

"Someone tried to run her off the road," Spencer said and looked over both shoulders. "I was there, I saw the whole thing. I got the plate number and gave it to Sparrow. I can't tell you what I know, other than what I already told you. The only bad thing about all of this is that Noreen was hurt because of me."

"Why you?" Mattie asked in genuine confusion.

"I think someone is after me. Someone from my

past. Don't say anything to anyone, please. I've got Stone and Swede from the Brotherhood Protection Agency working on it."

"Well, since I'm married to one of them, then I know you're in good hands. I'll keep quiet. What can we do for our girl here? What can I do to help?"

"Chloe just placed our lunch order, we'll take that home and eat. The doctor gave her the rest of the week off. She only has what you see in bruises, and I'm sure there are some you can't see. The good news is that there's nothing broken or bleeding internally, it's all surface damage. If you could give her the rest of the week to recuperate, that would be great."

"Done, report to work at ten Monday morning. If you don't feel better, call me by eight and I'll work my magic to get someone in to cover for you."

"Thanks Mattie. Thank you for being so under-standing."

"I would be heartless if I wasn't," Mattie said and grabbed the order pad from her apron pocket, and the pen from her hair. She quickly ripped off a page, wrote on it, then handed it to Spencer. "This is the number here at the restaurant, my personal cell, and my home number. If you need anything, and I mean anything, don't hesitate to call. Even if it's to bring you something to eat, or to come sit with her and Chloe if you can't be there." She passed him the paper and they looked up when Deanna came out, carrying a bag with take-out containers in it. She elbowed her way to Noreen, and winced when she saw how bruised her face was.

"Please tell me the other guy looks worse than you."

"I'm afraid not," Noreen shook her head then winced. As Deanna looked at Spencer, she passed him the bag.

"On the house, call if you need anything else, and one of us can run it out to you. You'll be staying with them to keep an eye on her?"

"I will." Spencer nodded and passed the food to Chloe when she joined them. He opened the door for her and grinned when she rolled her eyes at him. He also noted the women nodded in approval. He passed her the bag of food, and after Mattie and Deanna said their goodbyes, he climbed into the truck and left them staring after them.

When they arrived at Noreen's, Spencer opened the doors for them, then picked Noreen up and didn't set her down until they were at the door. He automatically took the keys from Chloe, and disappeared inside the house. He heard Chloe tell his mother what he was doing, and when he returned, he picked Noreen up and carried her directly to the living room and settled her in the corner of the couch. He even went as far as covering her legs with the quilt on the back of the couch. Between him and Chloe, they had their lunch ready in record time. No one said a word as they ate. It surprised Spencer that

Noreen ate as much as she had. It wasn't all of it, but she was able to eat half a sandwich and all of her fries. He asked what she wanted to drink besides the water, and he readily went to fix a cup of tea for her. He didn't return to the living room until he had both her tea and his coffee. He settled the drink on the table close to her, then settled in a chair across the room from mother and daughter, who sat on each end of the couch.

"Out with it, Barnes," Noreen said. "You have something to say, so say it."

CHAPTER 17

SPENCER LOOKED at the two women who stared at him with trusting eyes and heaved a gigantic breath. "To be honest, I'm kind of scared. I can only hope once you learn the truth, you won't kick me to the curb. I'm not afraid of saying this in front of Chloe, because I believe in honesty, but I really like you Noreen. I'm serious about what I told you the other day. I want to see if we can have a serious relationship, but I'm afraid you're going to kick me out after you learn what I have to say."

"Are you married?" Chloe asked, then looked at her mother. "Or do you have a secret family stashed somewhere and are just playing with my mother?"

"No, I'm not married, nor have I ever been. I'll tell you the same thing I told your mother. I've never been in a serious relationship before. Everything I had in the past didn't last longer than a night."

Chloe shrugged. "I'm good with that. What do you have to tell us?"

Spencer drew in a deep breath, held it for a long time, then let it out slowly. To stall, he sipped his coffee before he settled back in his chair. "I'm not being evasive, but there are some things I cannot reveal to you. I will tell you as much as I can, but don't get upset if I can't answer all of your questions. I'm saying this because there are some deep military secrets I'm talking about here. You could only know about them on a need-to-know-basis, and well, you two don't need to know." He paused to see how they would react.

"Okay," Noreen said as she turned to face him. She picked up her cup of tea and cradled it in her hands. "I'm good with that."

"Okay, as I told you before, I was in the military for twenty-three years. I'm currently forty-one years old. Three years after joining the Navy, I applied to SEAL training. I was accepted and went through six weeks of hell for my training."

"Is it anything like you see on TV?" Chloe asked in fascination.

"Worse," Spencer said and saw they understood. "I passed, and worked my way up to be a member of SEAL Team 6. That means that only the best of the best was accepted to that team. I worked on that team for years. There has been a group of special military personnel working for a special group. I can't give particulars, but know that only the best of the best is asked to join JSOC."

"What's that?" Noreen asked.

"It stands for Joint Special Operations Command. Like I said, only the best of the best is asked to join. However, it's not something you are part of all the time, like with SEAL Team 6. It's where a group of military personnel go in and perform a certain task. Once the assignment is done, you go back to your own team."

"Can you go back on it when another special assignment comes up again?" Chloe asked.

"Yes, that's how I got to be good friends with the men you met today. We were on several of these special assignments together. Where I was a member of SEAL Team 6, Darius, Simon, and Logan were Delta Force. Nash was a Ranger. The technical name for what they did is Army's 1st Special Forces Operation Detachment-Delta. That's what the first three I mentioned were. Nash was Army's Ranger Regimental Reconnaissance Company."

"They were Army and you were Navy?"

"Yes, and though they weren't on our team, the Air Force has been known to be called in to work a JSOC assignment right along with the rest of us. What I need to tell you is that the five of us along with three other members of my SEAL Team were on an assignment. Because of the nature of the assignment, I can't tell you where it was, or why we were there. I can tell you that, and please pardon my language, but I can tell you that it was a total goat fuck from the minutes we went wheels up."

"What's that?" Chloe asked as she settled back in the couch cushions and worked her bare feet beneath the blanket over her mother's lap. Spencer smiled when Noreen moved the blanket to give her more of it. He sipped his coffee to get his thoughts together before continuing.

"Wheels up means when the airplane leaves the tarmac and well, the wheels come off the ground."

"Oh, that's simple enough."

"Right," he chuckled as he sipped his coffee again. "Anyway, before we went wheels up, we were told what our mission was to be. When we landed and got to the location of the assignment, the person in charge gave us totally different orders. When we questioned him, he became belligerent toward us. It's not the first time we worked with this person, and it's not the first time he's tried to fuck us over."

"How did he do that?" Noreen asked as she stretched her legs out on the couch.

"Giving us false information. Threating our careers if we didn't go along with what they told us to do, or even questioned our orders. This person wasn't in the military, but he was high up in the government. Being a member of JSOC meant we had to follow his orders." Spencer shook his head and sipped his coffee again. Finding the cup empty, he jumped to his feet and went to refill it. When he returned, he set his cup down, but didn't sit back down himself. He paced as he gathered his thoughts and then turned fully to the two staring at him.

"Again, I can't tell you about the assignment, but we followed orders the best to our ability. Our target got away, but we were able to gather the information we were sent in to collect. Then all hell broke loose. We found a very important person in our location and we were told by people back home to protect him at all costs. If our mission for JSOC was under control, then get this person to safety. We did both." At their confused looks, he nodded. "Did our JSOC mission and protected this person. When all hell broke loose, we got him to safety, but found three of our buddies had been killed in the gun fight. They were men I served with on my SEAL Team for years. I took it hard." He paused and scrubbed his face, and turned his back on the women to get himself under control. When he felt like he had a handle on his emotions, he turned back to them. Their looks of understanding eased the tightness in his chest that had been there for months. "On the way home, the man in charge berated us for going off the books, his words, not ours, to help protect this particular person. We didn't know what he had done until we landed back in the States. We were met with some heavy-duty Brass." At their frowns, he nodded.

"Brass is what we called the top people in the

military. Anyway, we were met by them and told to go to a certain location. We thought it was an ordinary debriefing. That's where we tell our story to the higher-ups and they tell us what we can and can't say about the mission. This normally took only a few hours. This time it took days. Afterward, the five of were hit with devastating news." He walked over and sipped his coffee again, and settled back in his chair. He realized his hand was shaking in remembered anger. He wiped it down the thigh of his jeans several times to try to calm down.

"It still pisses me off. We learned that when we were being debriefed, The Fuckwad, that's what I call him. The man who was in charge over there. Anyway, The Fuckwad was telling the Brass lies about us. It was so bad that the Brass pressed charges against us."

"What happened?" Both women asked at the same time.

"We were called on the carpet, and in the ensuing months, based on The Fuckwad's lies, we were stripped of our careers." Spencer was so bitter he didn't see the two people on the couch wince at his tone, and look at each other in concern for the man sitting across from them. They knew he wasn't in the room with them as he continued talking.

"It took months for the hearing, but in the end the five of us were issued what they call an other-than-honorary discharge from our branches of the service.

Because of The Fuckwad's lies, our careers ended. We lost our pensions, along with our benefits. Hell, if we get sick, we can't even go to the local VA to get help. We have to go to a civilian doctor." He sat there for a long time looking at the floor. When he looked up a grin came over his face that caused both Noreen and Chloe to shudder.

"What?" Noreen asked.

Spencer drew in a deep breath and let it out slowly. "In recent months there have been some developments that are in our favor."

"How so?"

"It turns out that someone on the committee that stripped us of our careers did some digging and came up with proof that The Fuckwad lied to not only his superiors, but to ours in our different branches of the military. Based on what was uncovered he is now sitting in jail. He was denied bail, and has to stay there until the military gets to the bottom of things." Spencer shook his head and took up his coffee cup, cradling it next to his chest after taking a sip.

"Based on the information uncovered, The Fuckwad could possibly face charges of Treason."

"Holy crap, he lied that much?"

"Yes, see he destroyed the orders he gave us, then lied that they had never been available to us. Since getting out, that's why if I see something incriminating, I videotape it. That's why I taped what Jennifer was doing to you, Noreen. That's also why I taped what Brandi did to that girl in school. I told the entire student body that I had been bullied, and that's exactly what The Fuckwad did to us. He bullied us out of our careers. He used threats, intimidation, and outright lies to get rid of us."

"Why would he want to get rid of you?" Noreen asked in confusion. "I've followed everything you said, but why would he want to eliminate you?"

"Because he hated that the eight of us went in, did our job, was successful, then left. I guess you could say that in a nutshell, he was jealous that we could get the job done in hours, or sometimes days, while he couldn't. It galled him to have to call us in to do the job. But," Spencer smiled evilly at the two women. "Things have changed and are looking good for us."

"Can you tell us what it is?" Chloe asked.

"So far, Simon and indirectly, I have been attacked. I say indirectly because they tried to get me using your mother. I saw what happened to cause her accident, and it wasn't an accident. Someone hit her from behind and pushed her into oncoming traffic. Luckily, the other driver was smart enough to get out of the way, but your mother was pushed into a small ravine. She ended up at least twenty-five feet down. If I or the other driver hadn't seen it, no one would have seen her truck from the road. She could have been there for days. My story, as well as the other driver's were similar with on another. It helped that I caught a glimpse of the driver and was able to get his license plate."

"Wow, why do I have a feeling there's more to the story than what you're saying?"

"There is. While they were working on getting you out of your truck last night, I had Sparrow call her husband and another man he works with to the scene."

"Stone was there?"

"He was. See, when someone shot at Simon and Jocelyn a couple of months back, he hired Swede to look into the matter. It turns out that while we were on that mission that was a goat fuck from wheels up, The Fuckwad hired some very bad assassins to take us out. As in kill us off. He hated us that much. Anyway, one of those people are here, and based on what I saw, and what the Brotherhood has been able to uncover, The Fuckwad is neck deep in this shit."

"How?"

"It turns out he owns the shell company that hired the men to take us out. He is also in charge of the company that rented the vehicle that ran your mother off the road. With what was uncovered from the plate at your accident, there's someone with a lot of clout helping us by turning that information over to the proper authorities. The Fuckwad will do anything in his power to eliminate us. Why he has such hatred toward us, we'll never know. But," he grinned and the women shuddered again at his look. "It looks like we're going to have the last laugh."

"How?"

"Last week I received a certified letter that the military is looking further into our discharge. They openly admitted to us that they based their findings on what The Fuckwad told them. Since he's now sitting in jail because of the lies that were uncovered regarding his testimony about us, they are looking into the matter. It's good for us because we didn't go to jail."

"And it's bad for him because someone took the time to uncover the truth about his lies," Noreen said.

When Chloe started to chuckle the two adults looked at her in confusion. She looked at her mother with a grin. "Don't get upset, but I'm about to swear." She tuned to Spencer with another grin. "I can see it now, The Fuckwad thought everything was coming up roses when he had you guys kicked out of the military. Now he's sitting in jail, and if the military reinstates what you lost and what did you call it? Overturn your other-than-honorary discharge to an honorary one and you get your benefits and pension back, then wouldn't that be a final fuck you to The Fuckwad? He's sitting there in jail and you guys still come out smelling like roses. Can I ask why he's sitting in jail? What are his charges?"

"Once the person on the committee started digging around, they have proof he hired the people that attacked us and that very important person I told you about. They have records of money transfers from his personal accounts. Based on that information, he was charged with Treason as well as three counts of murder. That's for our teammates that didn't make it back alive." He looked at her intently. "See, the person that did the digging concluded that if he hadn't hired those people, then our target wouldn't have gone aground, it was discovered he paid the person we were there to protect to leave ahead of time. But if he hadn't hired those people to come at us with guns blazing, then Joe, Miquel, and Harry would still be alive today."

"Oh, wow. When will you know if you get your status back?"

"Not until The Fuckwad is convicted of his charges. Right now, he's sitting in Leavenworth without bail."

"If he's convicted what would happen to him? Would he get the death penalty?"

"He could, but he could also be sent to prison for no less than five years with a hefty fine. Don't forget, he'll have the three murder charges against him also." The three of them sat there in silence for several minutes before Noreen looked at Spencer with concern written all over her face.

"What about the guy that ran me off the road? What do we do about him?"

Spencer stood and pulled his phone out of his

pocket and walked over to the couch. He sat on the coffee table as he accessed the video he had taken of Jennifer stealing Noreen's tips. He paused it and turned the phone for both of them to look at. "This is Nate Renaldo. He is the hired gun sent by The Fuck-wad. Have you ever seen him before?"

Noreen took the phone and studied the photo of the man sitting in a booth in her section of the diner. She shook her head after several silent moments, and passed the phone to Chloe. "No, I've never seen him before. Why do you think he targeted me?"

"Don't quote me on this, but I think he might have been in the right place at the right time. He might have been sitting there quietly eating when I walked in. That was the day I met you, and if you recall, by the end of the day I had asked you out for a date. We set it up to meet at Gunny's a couple of days later. I don't know if he overheard us or what. That's the assumption I'm going on. I would bet he was the one that slashed your tires." Spencer took his phone back from Chloe and looked at her with a raised brow. When she denied seeing the other man, he believed her. As he stood, he studied the two of them intently.

"I don't mean to scare you, but I want the two of you to be extremely careful. With your permission, I'd like to contact the Brotherhood Protection Agency to come over and install a security system. I'm going to be staying here until you are able to get around better, Noreen. I would feel safer that both of you would have the security of the alarm while I'm at work." When it looked like she was about to protest what he was saying, he held up his hand.

"I will pay for it, and you can pay me back when you get a little extra money." He walked over to the table with his coffee cup, picked that up, along with the folder he had placed there and came back to sit on the low table again. He opened the folder and together, the three of them discussed which alarm systems would work the best for them. Spencer made the call to Jake to order it and was assured that someone from his agency would be there the next day to install it.

CHAPTER 18

Spencer ran through the rain, put his packages down, pounded on the door, and ran back for the rest of his things. By the time he returned to with the last load, Noreen and Chloe had opened the door and brought in the first batch of items. He hurried into the house, set his things down, then toed off his shoes. He looked at Noreen with a smirk when she handed him a towel so he could dry off.

"What's all this," she asked as she picked up a few of the bags and headed toward the kitchen. Spencer was close on her heels with the rest of them.

"I stopped and picked up some groceries. I don't know about you, but I'm getting sick of take-out. Not that the diner doesn't have great food, but having them deliver stuff is getting old. All day today, I could only think about a baked potato, a large steak, and a side salad. On the way home, I stopped at the store and might have gone a little overboard." He laughed when the two of them shook their heads at him.

"Might have?" Chloe asked as she opened a bag and brought out three different flavors of ice cream. "At least you got each of us our favorite flavors." They all shared a laugh as they continued to put away the groceries. He couldn't believe how good it felt to be with Noreen and Chloe every day. It was like they were a real family. The day after he brought Noreen home from the hospital, several members of The Brotherhood Protection agency showed up at her house bright and early. They assured him they would be there all day until he got home. They had installed the alarm system, and when he got home at nine that night, after his martial arts class, they went through the system with him, and had left. Spencer felt better leaving the two people important to him alone while he went to work. All day he had been thinking of how to bring up the fact that he didn't want to return to his lonely barren apartment after living there for the past week. He looked over at the two and started to say something, but the phone rang at the same time the doorbell peeled.

"I'll get the door," he said as Chloe ran to answer the house phone. He strode to the door and as soon as he opened it, it took only two seconds for him to go into action. He grabbed the hand that was aimed at him, twisted the wrist to the side, bending the thumb backward, then brought the person who aimed the gun at him to the ground. While doing this, the person who rang the doorbell screamed at the top of her lungs.

"What in the world?" Noreen asked as she ran to the door to see what all the commotion was. Chloe was right there beside her. Spencer heard her tell the person on the other end of the line that she would call them right back. The next thing he heard was Chloe talking to someone saying there was an intruder at their place.

"I called 9-1-1," she said to Spencer after she hung up the phone. "What's going on?"

"No clue, I opened the door and had a gun pointed at my chest," Spencer said as he took the belt Noreen handed him and tied the hands of the screaming offender. He flipped them over and swore when he saw Jennifer Lockwood staring back at him.

"What are *you* doing here?" Noreen demanded, then looked up when they heard sirens in the distance. No one said a word as the police vehicle pulled into the driveway, with another one parking on the street. The two people that rushed to the scene would know what was going on. Sheriff Faulker looked at the situation and demanded.

"What's going on?"

"The doorbell rang, I opened the door," Spencer said as he looked between the sheriff and his deputy, Sparrow. "As soon as I opened it, I had a gun pointed to my chest." He helped Jennifer to her feet, holding her hands behind her back as he pointed to the ground.

"It's a toy," Jennifer insisted, and they all watched as Faulker put on a pair of gloves, bent down and picked up the gun. He turned it over in his hands, and nodded.

"It is a toy, but it's still considered a lethal weapon when you pointed it at him."

"I didn't, he's lying. Just like he lied about my stealing money from the restaurant." Jennifer screamed. "Besides, he wasn't supposed to be here."

"You were going to shoot me?" Noreen asked in shocked surprise. "Why? I never did anything to you."

"You got me fired, you bitch! I had to spend almost a week in jail because of you!"

"No," Sheriff Faulkner said. "You got yourself fired, the video Mr. Barnes took of you proved it." He looked at Spencer with a scowl. "I see you have a doorbell with a camera on it, care if we access the footage?"

"Come on in," Spencer said, then looked at Noreen with a raised brow. She nodded and backed up. With Jennifer in tow, they all stepped inside the house, out of the rain. Sparrow waited just inside the door with Jennifer. She had put a set of cuffs on her, and returned the belt Spencer had used to restrain her. While the others went to view what the doorbell camera revealed, Sparrow read Jennifer her rights.

It didn't take long for the sheriff to return and he

held up a thumb drive. "It's just as Spencer said. He opened the door, she lifted her hand with a gun in it. Even though it's a toy, it's still considered attempted murder." No one said a word as Jennifer started screaming and tried to get away from Sparrow. The deputy took her to the floor, and as she was brought back to her feet, there were charges of resisting arrests being talked about. Sparrow led the screaming woman away, and the Sheriff stayed behind.

"Thank you for you quick action, Barnes." He turned to Noreen. "I'm glad you didn't answer the door, or you," he said as he turned to Chloe. "Though the weapon is a toy, it's still a weapon and there's no telling what would have happened if you two ladies had been here alone. We're taking Ms. Lockwood to the jail to book her on attempted murder and resisting arrest. I have to ask, would you like to press charges against her?"

Noreen looked around wildly, then sighed in relief when her daughter stepped up to her side, wrapped her arm around her waist, and asked, "Will it carry more weight if we do?"

"It will. The video clearly shows her intent to do harm. I would highly recommend you come down to the station and give me a report."

"Can I do it here?" Noreen asked. She pointed to her wildly colored face and grimaced. "I really don't want to go out in public if I don't have to. I'm sure I'll be fine on Monday, but I'd like to stay hidden if I can."

"I understand," the sheriff said and talked into his radio. He told Sparrow to take the suspect to the station and book her. He also said he was going to get statements from the occupants. It took well over an hour, but he did his job and told them to come down to the station when they had a chance to sign their statements. He should have then typed up by then. After the sheriff left, Spencer looked at the two women and he did the only thing he could think of. He opened his arms wide, and sighed in relief when they both rushed him. He closed them all in a hug and they stayed like that for some time. Chloe was the first one to break away.

"Holy shit," she said and shook her head at her mother, who mirrored her sentiment. "That would have been scary if we had been home alone."

"I know," Noreen said as she shuddered. She went to the kitchen and the first thing she did was grab the tea kettle to fill. Spencer knew that when she drank a cup of tea, it was only when she was upset and needed to calm down. To distract the others, he looked at Chloe.

"Who was that on the phone?"

"Oh, that was Mr. Dickson, he wanted to know if he and Brandi could come over and talk with me."

"What for?" Noreen asked from her position by the stove, then widened her eyes at her daughter. "Do you think it might be to discuss what happened to her?"

"I don't know. Before I hung up on him, he asked me if I knew how to get ahold of Spencer. He said he called The Centre, but only got the answering machine."

"Well, it is closed until Monday," Spencer said with a smirk, and the two of them shook their head at him. "Call him back and tell him to come over. No offense, Chloe, but if Brandi is going to apologize to you, or reveal what bug crawled up her ass, then she needs to do it on your turf."

"Why?"

"Because it will throw her off her game if she has to do it in a place she's not familiar with."

"Is that so she won't cop an attitude if I don't agree with what she has to tell me."

"Yes." Spencer nodded as he went over to the stove an turned the fire off beneath the screaming kettle. He looked at Noreen, and without any words, he stepped up behind her and wrapped his arms around her. When she turned and wrapped her arms around his waist, and placed her head in the center of his chest, all was right with his world.

"I'll call him back," Chloe said quietly as she picked up the phone and dialed. Three minutes later she looked at them after hanging up the phone. "Mr. Dickson said they would be here in thirty minutes."

Noreen stepped away from Spencer to begin to

make a fresh pot of coffee, while Chloe got out some of the cookies Spencer had bought earlier. By the time the knock came at the door, they were ready for guests. Noreen and Chloe had no problem letting Spencer go to the door. This time, before he opened it, he looked through the peep hole. He had forgotten that Stone had told them they installed on while they had put in the security system. He opened the door to two solemn looking people.

"Mr. Dickson, Brandi," Spencer said by way of greeting and stepped back. He saw Brandi immediately remove her shoes, and knew she must have been there often enough in the past to know the rules of the house. He thought back to what had happened two hours ago and chuckled to himself that he had taken Jennifer down in his sock feet. Shaking his head, he invited them in, and stopped when Brandi sucked her breath in hard and gave a little screech.

"Mom Noreen, what happened to you?" She rushed forward, but stopped short before she reached her.

"I'm fine, Brandi. I'm actually on the mend. I was in a car accident and this is the results."

"Oh," Brandi said. As it became awkward, Noreen passed out cups of coffee and juice for the girls. They took themselves into the living room. When no one said anything for some time, it was Spencer that got the ball rolling.

"What brings you here, Mr. Dickson?"

Spencer liked that the other man didn't beat around the bush. He was direct and to the point. "I'd like to apologize to you for my actions that day. There's no excuse for what I did. I know now that I didn't have all the information when I attacked you. Brandi knows what I did to you, and why I did it. After talking with you, we finally sat down and had a heart-to-heart that was a long time coming." He drew in a deep breath and let it out slowly. After taking a sip of his coffee, he looked at the others, nodded once, and began.

"I know it's not an excuse, but I thought not talking to Brandi about my separation from her mother was protecting her. I hadn't realized that keeping facts and truths from her would hurt her, or cause her to strike out at her friends." He turned to Chloe then. "I'm really sorry she did that to you."

"Dad, I can speak for myself," Brandi said as she too turned to Chloe. "I'm sorry for being such a bitch to you. Will you allow me to tell you what happened, and why I acted the way I did?"

"Yes," Chloe said as she grabbed a cookie and settled back in her chair. "I'm ready."

Brandi grinned, then quickly sobered. "Dad probably won't like what I'm going to say, or how I'm going to say it, but it's the only way I can express myself." She looked at Noreen and nodded only once. "Forgive me, but I'm going to swear."

Noreen nodded and gripped Chloe's hand in hers. "I understand."

They all watched as Brandi drew in a deep breath and let the air out in a rush, along with her words. "My mother is an alcoholic crack whore." When her father didn't say anything to stop her, she continued. "I saw Mom over the Christmas break. I hadn't seen or heard from her since she left. Dad wouldn't talk about the separation, and all the time she was gone, I thought it was all my fault. I had overheard them fighting about me before she left. As you know, my siblings are several years older than me and away at college. Before she left, I overheard Mom scream at Dad that if she hadn't had me, then all her problems would go away."

"Shit." This time it was Noreen who swore. "I hope your line of thinking changed."

"It did, as soon as I saw her during Christmas break, I knew all her problems were in her head. See, when I talked to her on the phone after she left, she was always so upbeat and happy. She spun the fabulous life she had. I couldn't wait to see her during the break. The reality is that she lives in flop houses. She doesn't have a permanent home, and she's only happy and upbeat when she's high. I was supposed to spend three days with her, but I only lasted one. I called dad to come get me the next day. See, we were in a homeless shelter that first night, and someone there tried to rape me. I was able to fight him off, and the bitch of it was, that Mom knew the man. He was her dealer and she told him he could have me if she could score drugs from him. When I fought him off, he threatened Mom's life. I didn't know what to do. I didn't sleep the entire time, and I called Dad the minute the sun was up the next day.

"I became increasingly scared over the next few weeks when Mom would call and try to convince me that I owed her. That if I loved her I would do what her dealer wanted. He wanted to pimp me out, those where his words to me. After about three phone calls, I started ignoring her number when it came across my screen. Oh, I would listen to the voicemails, but I never talked to her. As time went by, the messages became more and more threatening, and I became more and more scared. Petrified at times that this guy was going to find me and force me to do what Mom said he would. She even told me that she told him where I lived."

"Why didn't you come to me with this?" Chloe asked in shocked dismay as she leaned forward and reached out to her. Brandi gripped her hand, and when she looked up, she had tears streaming down her face. "I would have helped you."

"Honestly?"

"Always."

"I was jealous."

"Of what?"

"You."

"Chloe?" Noreen asked in shock.

"Actually, it's both Chloe and you Mom Noreen. It's not you individually, but the relationship you have with one another. I always wanted that with my mother, but I always felt like I never lived up to her expectations. Why do you think I never wanted you over to my house, Chloe? Sure, you'd come over a lot, but I always made sure she wasn't there when you visited. I loved coming here because of your relationship. I felt I got at least some maternal love by watching the two of you." She reached up and wiped her tears, then gave a soggy laugh when both Noreen and Chloe rushed to hug her.

Once they settled back down, Brandi looked at her father. Spencer noted he gave her a subtle nod. Brandi turned to the three of them. "Mr. Barnes, I'm sorry for what I told my dad about the videotape you took of me bullying that girl on the day of the assembly. I lied and manipulated my dad to get that video from you. When he came home and told me what he saw and demanded answers, I realized I was turning into my mother and I got scared. I told him everything, I even saved the voicemails and let him hear them."

"What did you do about them?" Spencer demanded.

"Because my soon-to-be-ex-wife lives in Colorado Springs, I went there to talk to their police force. I contacted Sheriff Faulkner first to see who I should talk to. I can't get into the specifics, but we are pressing charges against her and her pimp."

"After talking to the police over there, he recommended I get counseling and he even gave us a business card of someone. We called them before we left the parking lot and was able to get right in to see her. I'm in counseling two times a week. It's only been a week so far, and I'm far from healed, but I feel better to be able to talk to someone about what I experienced. I don't know if I will ever have the desire to see my mother face-to-face again, but it's something I'm working on." Everyone was quiet for a few minutes before Brandi turned all her attention to Chloe.

"Chloe Rafferty, I am sorry for the way I treated you these last few months. I have no excuse for my behavior. I know it's a lot to ask, but when you feel it's right, I would like to be friends with you again."

Spencer winced at her wording, and Tom must have garnered the same feeling because he only said one word, "Brandi."

"Sorry," the other girl sighed. "I know that was putting too much pressure on you."

"It is," Chloe said with conviction. "Brandi, I never stopped being *your* friend. *You* were the one to push me away. I'm not saying I won't be your friend again, but I think you need to work on you first. The only thing I can say is that we need to take it one day at a time and see how that goes."

"I'll accept that," Brandi said and lunged for the other girl. Spencer felt his own eyes moisten when he saw the joy on the two young faces. He coughed and got up to refill their coffee mugs, but Tom said it was time for them to go. After they left, Spencer studied Chloe closely, then walked up to her and wrapped her into a hug.

"I'm proud of you."

"Thank you," she said as she hugged him back, then kissed his cheek. "Did I hear mention something about a steak?" They all laughed as they made their way to the kitchen and cooked the evening meal as a family.

CHAPTER 19

"I MEAN IT," Spencer glowered down at Chloe with his fisted hands on his hips. "Call me the minute you get home."

"Mom," Chloe looked at her mother as she whined.

"He's just looking out for your safety, Chloe," Noreen said with a smile to her daughter. When it looked like she would argue more, Noreen leaned in to say in a loud whisper. "Don't worry, he's already made me promise to call him on my breaks."

"I promise this won't last forever, I just want to keep my girls safe. Once the asshat hired by The Fuckwad is caught, then I might ease up on my demands."

"Might?" Both of them asked as one with a heavy dose of smiles aimed at him.

Spencer felt his cheeks turn hot, but only shrugged as he continued to look at Chloe.

"Fine, I promise to call you when I get home."

"Thank you," Spencer said as he picked up his travel mug and made his way to the door. He paused to dress his feet, then the three of them left together. Since Noreen hadn't heard back from the insurance company about her vehicle yet, she had talked with Mattie and had her hours changed so that Noreen could work the same hours Spencer did, allowing him to drop her off and pick her up. Today they happened to both have to go in early, and Chloe had asked for a ride to school.

In the drop off lane at the school, Chloe rolled her eyes and Spencer parked, got out, then came around to the side of the truck and opened her door. She still didn't know how she felt about it, but when she got out and saw the cool girls looking at Spencer like he was a fresh slab of meat for them to devour, she stepped up to him and kissed his cheek. He chuckled in her ear, and with a grin, she left him, but not before promising to call when she got home. Spencer watched as the girls that had ogled him converged on Chloe the second she stepped up onto the walk heading to the school.

"You just made her day," Noreen laughed as he climbed back in the truck and drove back to town. He only looked at her and rolled his eyes. Something he'd seen Chloe do several times. Noreen burst out laughing. He pulled into the back of the diner and did the same thing with Noreen as he had with Chloe. He got out and went to open her door. Except with her, he stopped her and leaned in to give her a long kiss.

"Something to hold you over until tonight."

"Thanks," she sighed and shook her head. "Maybe tonight we can resume our sex life."

"Promise?"

"Maybe, if you're a good boy."

"I will be," he grinned and kissed her again. Since her accident, he hadn't wanted to touch her other than hold her while she slept. She had been sore and severely bruised and he didn't want to aggravate her pain by asking for sex. When she'd felt better, she'd gotten her period and they had to wait another week. As she walked away from him, he slapped her ass and laughed when she only shook her head at him. He wore a grin all the way to The Centre.

"Barnes," Spencer barked into his phone. He had been running since he entered The Centre hours ago, and hadn't really had the time to stop. With all the students and parents that wanted to take his self-defense classes, he had been swamped. One good thing about the entire process was when Chloe had mapped out a schedule for him. He found if he followed it, he didn't get confused, and he knew which class he would be teaching next.

"Hello? Is anybody there?" Spencer demanded and had to strain to hear the voice on the other end of the line. "Chloe?" He immediately looked at his watch and saw it was around the proper time she was due home.

"Spencer," came the whispered voice. "Someone's in the house."

"What did you say?" Spencer froze at the words, then his military training kicked in. "Where are you right this minute? What room of the house are you in?"

"My bedroom."

"Not that I don't trust you, but how do you know someone's in the house?"

"I heard something break downstairs, I think it's a window." Before she even finished her sentence there was a loud piercing sound coming over the phone. He knew it was the alarm, and that someone had breached the house. He turned on his heel and ran to Simon's office.

"Chloe, can you get to the attic without being seen?"

"I think so, why?"

"There's a truck up there, a big one. I put it there myself last weekend. Go to the attic, and climb into that truck. It's big enough for you to fit inside. Don't come out until you hear from me. I'm sure if the alarm didn't scare the guy off, the police will be on their way. Now go." He waited as he saw his buddies in Simon's office.

"Simon, how many weapons do you have here at The Centre?"

"Why?"

"Someone broke into the house, and Chloe's home alone."

"Shit," Simon said as he jumped to his feet and unlocked a cabinet in the corner of his office. As soon as it was open, Darius, Nash, Logan, and Simon all reached in for the guns of their choice. Simon passed Spencer the weapon he preferred.

"I'm here," Chloe said. "I didn't see anyone, but I can hear them over the alarm."

"I'm on my way, Chloe. I promise I will get to you. You have to promise me you won't come out until you hear from me, and only me."

"I promise." Came the small reply. "Can I keep my phone line open?"

"Yes, I'll keep mine open too. You'll be hearing a lot of talk on my end, but that's me coordinating your rescue with others. Please, do not talk unless you are in immediate danger."

"I promise," Chloe said. "Hurry."

Spencer winced at the fear he heard in his voice. He left the phone on, but stuck it in his shirt pocket. As he donned the flak vest handed to him, he updated the others on the situation. Darius hung up the phone and nodded to him.

"I called Jake, he's sending a crew over to meet us."

"Good," Spencer said and frowned as Nash scribbled something on a piece of paper, slapped it on the front door, and the five of them hurried out to their trucks. As he looked back, Spencer saw that Nash had written 'closed' on the paper and locked the front door. They ended up taking only two trucks, and Spencer's tire threw rooster tails of gravel as he raced out of the parking lot. It took ten minutes to get to Noreen's house. He rounded the corner and had to slam on his brakes a few yards back because of all the police cars there.

Armed to the teeth, the five men rushed out of the trucks, and made their way to the sheriff. They had to slide the last few feet in when there were shots fired at them.

"Is that from inside the house?" Spencer demanded.

"Yes. Where's Noreen and Chloe?"

"Noreen's still at work. Chloe's upstairs in the attic. She called me when she heard broken glass. I had to go to the attic and hide inside a trunk." He pulled his phone and held it up. "Chloe, this is Spencer. Don't talk if you don't feel safe. We're outside, the police are here. Hang in there, we're coming. Are you still safe?"

"Yes," came the small voice, and Spencer's heart

cracked at the fear he heard. He looked up when they were joined by several heavily armed men, and he saw they were employees of The Brotherhood Protection Agency. He also saw Faulkner put his finger to his lips and point to the phone.

"What can you tell me?"

"Nothing, I'm in the truck like you told me. I hear a lot of crashing. Mom's going to be pissed at the mess."

Spencer chuckled. "We'll deal with your mother later. We can do it together. The most important thing is to make sure your safe. Were you able to close the attic door behind you?"

"Yes. It was hard, but I did it."

"Good girl. I'm going to talk strategy now. Hang in there, we're coming. I promise I'm coming." Spencer put the phone in his pocket and looked at the others. They were on the side of the road, and it wasn't paved, so he scuffed up the dirt at his feet. He used his hands to draw out the outline of the inside of the house.

"Where's Chloe?" Logan asked.

"Here, but she's in the attic. It's not a room you can open a door and walk up the stairs. You have to pull down the stairs to get to them. If you don't know where the entrance is, it's hard to find. That's why I sent her there."

"What trunk is she in?"

"My military foot locker." The other former military men gave him a thumbs up or a high-five on his choice of hiding spots for her. Suddenly there was the sound of breaking glass, and shots rang out again.

"That came from an upstairs window," Sparrow said as she hunkered down next to them. She pointed to the makeshift drawing and Spencer nodded.

"Hallway."

"How do you want to do this, Faulkner?" Stone asked the older man.

"I know I can't tell you guys to stand down, hell between all of you I'm betting you have over a hundred years military experience. I'm going to stay out here and coordinate with Cogburn. Spencer, you know the house, why don't you take your men and work you way to the back? Sparrow, grab a group of men and make your way to the front." Jim shook his head sadly. "I only hope Noreen has good insurance to replace all the broken glass and doors."

"I'm sure she does," Spencer said and he used his eyes and hands to lead his team to the back of the house. They had stopped long enough to fit themselves with ear wigs, and when he was in position, he told Sparrow they were ready. Into his shirt he whispered to Chloe that they were coming and to sit still, no matter what she heard. When he got the okay from her, he told Sparrow to breach the front. As soon as the front door was kicked in, so was the back door. Spencer entered Noreen's house like he had done other houses on other military missions. He couldn't let his personal feeling intrude on the job at hand. He ignored the items he saw in the house and looked in each room. When he met up with Spar-row's team at the base of the stairs, they paused when they heard glass break, and Spencer was the first one up the stairs. In his ear, he heard several people from the outside shout that there was a runner. He made it to the broken window in time to see a man limp across the field, by the time the people down below gave chase, the running man was driving away in a car.

"Fuck," Spencer swore, then he watched as the others cleared the rest of the house. As soon as he got the all clear, he walked down the hall, jumped up to grab the cord and pulled down the stairs. "Chloe, he said into his shirt. I'm coming up."

"Okay," came the small, terrified voice, and Spencer took the narrow stairs as fast as he could. He didn't know if he was grateful or not that Logan was right on his ass. He was grateful when Logan cleared the room, and Spencer did an impressive slide across the dusty floor to get to the truck. He whipped the lid open and reached in. As soon as he touched Chloe, she screamed but he kept he voice calm and in seconds she wrapped herself tightly around him, crying into his shoulder.

"Spencer, you came."

"I promised you I would." He gripped her hard, and didn't care that he had tears running down his face. He leaned back and took her face in his hands to study her intently. He kissed her forehead, and to lighten the mood, he smiled at her. "You did good, kid." Spencer looked to the side when Logan squatted down next to them.

"You did really good, kid," Logan said. "You should be proud of yourself. The first thing you need to do to keep safe in a situation like this is to listen to the man in charge. You did good by calling Spencer and then following his directions."

"And to think," Chloe shook her head at Spencer. "I argued with you this morning when you told me to call you when I got home."

"How much time passed from when you arrived home to when you heard the break-in?" Spencer asked as he helped Chloe to her feet, and nodded when Logan took their guns and went ahead of them.

"I'm sorry to admit that I forgot to call you. When I got home, I got something to drink and a snack. I had just gone into my room when I heard the glass break then I was on the phone with you when the alarm sounded. Probably ten minutes." When she was down from the attic, she scowled at him. "If we are up here, who turned off the alarm?" It had suddenly stopped screaming when Spencer had been holding her in the attic.

"Probably one of the guys who installed it," Logan said and kept the guns hidden from her view as much as possible. He left and Spencer slowly examined the damage left behind by the intruder. He met Sparrow in the downstairs, and wrapped his arm around Chloe at the destruction they found.

"Shit, Mom's going to be pissed."

Spencer and Sparrow shared a chuckle, and the deputy said the crime scene unit was on the way. They went outside and Spencer stood as close to Chloe as she would allow him as she gave her statement to Sparrow. He was grateful that Nash said he'd stay with Chloe while Spencer went to pick up Noreen from her job.

CHAPTER 20

"How was your day?" Spencer asked Noreen as soon as she climbed into the truck. He had been there with the door open, waiting for her. After a quick kiss, he went around to his side of the truck and climbed in. He did not start the truck up right away. He waited for her answer.

"Good, we weren't as busy as I thought we would be. But it was a good day. What about you? How was your day?"

"Eventful," Spencer said, but didn't elaborate as he played with the keys on his ring and stared out the windshield, afraid to look at her.

"Spencer, what's wrong? Don't tell me nothing, either. I can tell you have something to say, and it's bothering you."

Spencer drew in a deep breath, held it for several

seconds, and let it out slowly as he turned his entire body toward her. "Chloe called me after school."

"Okay, you had to drag a promise out of her, but I'm glad she did."

"Someone broke into the house after she got home. She called me in a panic, I told her where to hide. The guys and I grabbed weapons and went to the house. The alarm went off, and we called in Jake and the guys. When we arrived at the house, the police were there, and someone was shooting out at us."

"Chloe? Is Chloe okay?"

"She's fine, she did as I said immediately, and she was safe the entire time. Remember that foot locker I took to the attic last weekend?"

"Yes, what about it?"

"It's bullet proof. I had her hide in there."

Noreen sighed heavily and closed her eyes in relief. She opened them quickly to stare at him in horror. "Did you catch the guy?"

"No, but he was limping when I saw him tear out over the field. We did not fire upon him, all the gunshots were from him toward us. He must have hurt himself when he jumped out of the second story window. Nash and Julienne, his girlfriend is at the house with Chloe now. The guys stayed with us all afternoon and after Sparrow took her statement, the crime scene techs showed up. They left two hours ago, the guys and their women were helping Chloe clean up the mess."

"Can we do that? Doesn't the police need the house for evidence?"

"Already collected. That's what the crime scene techs did. They dusted for prints. You'll probably have to go in and give your for elimination purposes. Chloe already did hers. Mine are already on file."

"Before you take me directly to my daughter," Noreen glared at him as she said sternly. "What is your honest, gut rendering opinion. Who do you think did this?"

"Nate Renaldo. He fit the description of the man running away from the house. I would bet my left nut it was him. I don't know if he'll be back or not, he was limping pretty badly, he might have broken something, or severely sprained an ankle or knee. I want you to know that I will refer to your judgement. If you don't want to say in the house until we can replace the windows, we can go to a hotel or to my apartment. As Chloe said, the furnishings are a little sparce, but there's room for us."

"I'll withhold judgement until I see it with my own eyes. Now," she said firmly as she reached over and grabbed her seatbelt. She snapped it in place and nodded to him. "Take me to my daughter."

"Yes, Ma'am," Spencer said as he turned, and fired up the truck. Ten minutes later he pulled into the driveway and noted the same cars were there as when he'd left to pick Noreen up from work. He didn't admonish her when she didn't wait for him to open the door. She was out of the truck before he had shut off the engine. He couldn't blame her. He made his way behind her, and walked in the door to see her grab Chloe, turn her around, and engulf her in a hug."

"Mom, I'm fine. Spencer kept me safe the entire time. I had contact with him through our phones." It took some convincing, but Noreen finally backed off and looked around her home.

"We've cleaned most of it up," Chloe told her. "The guys went to the hardware store to get some plywood to put over the broken windows."

"How many of there are there?" Noreen refused to look at Spencer as she asked this.

"Three," Darius answered as he introduced himself and Fenmore to Noreen. "One upstairs, one at the back of this level. That's where we believe he broke in from. Then one of the front windows. That is where he was firing at us."

Noreen threw daggers at Spencer, and it was Logan who came up to her. "Ma'am, I don't remember if we met each other yet, but I'm Logan Bishop. I was with these men when we lost our military careers. Don't take your anger out of the asshat that did this on Spencer. He had nothing to do with it."

"Yes, he did. That asshat, as you called him, is after

Spencer. It seems like he's using me and my daughter to get to him. Not only did he slice my tires, but he's the one that ran me off the road. Now he's going after my daughter? That is unforgivable."

"Noreen," Fenmore said as she slowly approached. "I understand you're upset. I would be too if I had a child that was targeted. However, I have to tell you, I was on the committee that kicked these guys out of the service. I voted to allow them to be honorable discharged, I was overruled. Because of that, I did some digging and found evidence of lies Mathias used to get them kicked out."

"Who's Mathias?" Noreen frowned at her.

"The Fuckwad," Spencer said. "He doesn't deserve the name he was given at birth to be spoken out loud. We all refer to him as The Fuckwad."

"Okay, then," Fenmore chuckled. "Anyway, if you want to be pissed at anyone, be pissed at The Fuckwad."

"Yeah," Jocelyn said. "If it's the guy we think it is, he even shot at Simon and I when we came out of a restaurant over in Colorado Springs a few weeks ago. He wasn't caught then, and it looks like he wasn't caught this time either. From what I heard, he's hurting though. The men didn't have to act like they did, but they treated getting to Chloe like it was a mission they'd been on before. She was their primary goal, and they did everything within their power to take out Renaldo and get to Chloe."

"I was safe Mom. It's not Spencer's fault The Fuckwad has some sort of hard-on for these guys."

"Chloe!" Noreen stared at her daughter in shock, and then at the men and women who burst out laughing. She also noted that Spencer stood off to the side and thought he smiled at what her daughter said, it didn't reach his eyes.

"I'm sorry," he said, and the look on her face caused her to rush to him and throw her arms around his neck.

"No, I'm sorry for doubting that you would intentionally put my child in danger. Since you've been staying here, you have been nothing but supportive of both of us. I'm the one that is sorry."

Spencer sighed in relief as he wrapped his arms around her and buried his face in her neck. "I promise to keep both of you safe, or die trying," he said into her neck, for her ears only. They stayed like that for several minutes before Chloe called out,

"Hey, get a room why don't you. Oh, and speaking of the two of you getting a room, Spencer, can you do me a favor?"

Spencer grinned at Noreen as they turned toward Chloe with raised brows. "What's that?"

"Next time you and mom do the deed, can you not wear a condom?"

"CHLOE!" Noreen screeched at her daughter.

"Excuse me?" Spencer said in shock.

"This is getting good," Logan laughed and rubbed

his hands together. When no one said anything else, he looked at the young lady. "Why don't you want Barnes to glove up?"

Chloe wrinkled her nose at Logan but turned to her mother and Spencer. She looked them each in the eye and said as plain as day, "I want a sibling." She shrugged, and the others made their way to the front door, saying they were out of there. Logan laughed like a loon the entire way to the door.

"Lock up after us," he called out. Several moments later, he opened the door again and called into the room. "I said, lock up."

Spencer roused himself enough to walk to the door, push Logan's face out of the crack, then slammed the door shut and turned the lock. He turned to look at Noreen; she was looking at him, not at her daughter as he expected.

"I'm off to bed," Chloe said breezily, and she came up to him and kissed his cheek, thanked him again for saving her life, then hugged her mother, kissing her cheek. She was gone in seconds. It was like a whirlwind had passed through and taken all the oxygen out of the room with her.

"Well," Noreen said as she stared at Spencer, unsure of what to say next.

"Do you want me to leave?" Spencer asked and held his breath while he waited for her answer.

"No, but only if you want to. I won't hold you here."

"I want to stay."

"Then stay. I'm sorry I said what I did and reacted the way I did. I was scared for my daughter."

"I totally understand. I have to admit that when I finally got to her, I hugged her and cried like a little baby when I knew she was safe."

"Really?"

"Yes," Spencer said as he went to the kitchen and automatically began to clean up the mess from the pizza someone had ordered as they had all worked together to put Noreen's house back together. He saw where some black smudges from the fingerprint powder hadn't been removed lately, and shook his head. "I'll clean that up later."

"What?" Noreen asked in confusion, then scowled when he pointed to the mess. "What is it?"

"Fingerprint powder."

"Oh," she didn't say anything again until the kitchen had been put back to rights, then turned to him with a frown. "Question for you."

"Shoot."

"If they find the asshat's fingerprints in my house, can they be used against The Fuckwad in the case against him? I don't know, stating something like the asshat was hired by The Fuckwad, and he went after your family."

"Yes." Spencer didn't hesitate in his answers. "We can talk to Fenmore, and we can get the information to the proper people. The only thing we'll have to wait for is the results back from the crime lab. I'm sure Sparrow or Sheriff Faulkner will sent a copy of everything to the proper people." He looked at her and sighed heavily as he studied her.

"How good is your home owner's insurance?"

"No clue, I've never had to use it, but I'm sure, as you said, with the proper reports, I can open a claim and have these windows replaced."

"One good thing," Spencer chuckled as he approached her.

"What's that?"

"At least you might get a break when they learn you installed an alarm and it worked."

"There is that," Noreen shared a chuckle with him. She looked around and shook her head.

"What is it?"

"Do you think we'll be safe for the night?"

"I do, that is, if you don't mind having a gun on the bedside table beside us. I'll keep the safety on, but I'd feel better if my weapon is close at hand."

"Maybe you should teach me how to shoot, as well as lessons in self-defense. I'd like to be prepared as long as The Fuckwad has access to the outside world."

"I agree, but you'd be better off talking to Simon about lessons on weapons. He's our weapons guy."

"What do the others do?" Noreen asked as she waited at the base of the stairs for him to check the still-intact windows. As they walked up the stairs together, he explained. "Darius is our computer guy, he runs a lot of programs for other people, but he's been known to teach a class or two on how to program things and to troubleshoot your own computer. Simon is our weapons guy. He can teach you all about them and what would be best for you if you wanted to buy a gun for your own personal protection. Nash is our Zen guy." Spencer laughed at her expression of shock.

"What's that mean?"

"It means that he is so Zen that nothing seems to phase him. But when it comes to the point where we're on a mission, he's there, one hundred percent. He is in charge of all the Yoga classes at The Centre."

"And Logan?" Noreen asked as they entered the bedroom, and she saw that nothing had been disturbed in that room, causing her to breathe easier.

"Logan is our SERE guy. That means he trains people in survival, evasion, resistance, and escape. He likes to take his classes out into the woods and teach them there. That's where he's best suited. He's also a pilot. That's what he did while on the JSOC team. Now he does it for pleasure."

Noreen remained silent for a while, but Spencer saw she had nodded in acknowledgment. They quickly undressed, and because Spencer had been scared for Chloe's life, he had sweated a lot and wanted to jump in the shower to clean up. It didn't surprise him when Noreen joined him minutes later.

They didn't do anything in the shower except for washing one another, and Spencer withheld his smile when they crawled into bed, and Noreen hadn't put on her favorite sleeping outfit of shorts and a ratty tee shirt. She crawled between the sheets naked. He did too.

CHAPTER 21

AFTER HE SETTLED in the bed, he opened his arm and sighed in relief when she settled into his favorite spot for her to be in with her head on his shoulder and her hand on his lower stomach. He wrapped her arm around him and held her tightly for a few seconds.

"We good?"

"We are."

Spencer laid there for several minutes playing with Noreen's long hair and frowned when she sat up suddenly, then turned to look down at him. She grabbed a pillow to cover her nakedness.

"What's on your mind?" Spencer asked as he pushed himself up in the bed so his back rested against the headboard. He took the hand she offered him and liked that she entwined their fingers.

"Before we fall asleep, or do anything before we

fall asleep," she grinned at his expression, "I want to know what you thought of Chloe's comment?"

"About having a sibling?"

"Yes, I'll be the first to admit that it knocked me for a loop."

"Me too. I hate to even ask this, because I will be the first to admit that I have no clue how a woman's body works. Let alone their reproductive organs. Can you even still have children?"

"Yes, as long as I still get my period, I can get pregnant. The question is, do *you* want children? You haven't been in any type of serious relationship your entire life, and I wondered if that was because you didn't want children."

"It's not that," Spencer said as he studied her hand in his, then looked directly at her. "I lived for my career back then. Having it taken away from me, I realized that I might have wasted all that time where I could have had a family. But," he held up her hand to stop what she was about to say. "I know now, after being with you, that those other women weren't right for me for the long haul. They filled my need for a one and done, that was it. With you, it's entirely different. Also, with Chloe."

"I'm trying not to fish for compliments here, but what do you mean by that?"

"Marriage and children were never on my radar. Ever. Like I said, I lived, breathed, and ate the SEALs. Being a SEAL was my life. Looking back, I knew it wouldn't have been fair to any woman, or child I would have had to have any type of relationship. I hope I'm saying this right, but I would be out the door the minute I got the call. I wouldn't have given a wife or child a second thought until I walked back in the door. Since losing my career, and meeting you, it's different."

"How?"

"I can't wait to get home to both of you. I know I'm not Chloe's biological father, but I feel like I am her dad. I love what you and I have together. Both in and out of bed. I love talking with Chloe every night at the dinner table, to learn about her day. I also like watching her try to wake up in the mornings." He grinned when Noreen laughed along with him.

"Yeah, she's not a morning person."

"I know." Spencer shook his head, then turned serious. "I stayed the night of your accident to ease your mind about someone being here for her while you were laid up in the hospital. It was no hardship at all to do that. I stayed the next night to make sure you were still okay after your concussion."

"Is that why you woke me all the time that night to talk to me?"

"Yes, I wanted to make sure you were okay. I could have left to go back to my place the next night, but I stayed. Hell, I could have gone home anytime in the past two weeks, but I stayed. I stayed because I want to be with you, and through you, I feel like I'm a father for the first time with Chloe." He studied her intently for several silent moments.

"What?" she asked in concern.

"Don't hate me for this, but at least I missed the diaper stage, as well as the terrible two's."

Noreen stared at him in shock, then leaned over because she was laughing so hard. When she sobered, she wiped her happy tears and grinned at him. "Actually, Chloe was a pretty easy child. She was potty trained by eighteen months, she did most of it on her own."

"How did she do that?"

"I put a potty chair in the bathroom, and when I went, I'd bring her in and sit her down. Fully clothed, but after a couple of weeks, when I went to go to the bathroom, she would take off her bottoms and join me. I praised her, but didn't make a big deal of it. Within a couple of weeks, she was complete potty trained. The only hard part was getting her to use the big girl potty." She smirked and went on to tell him the first time she tried to use it by herself and fell in. They both ended up laughing until they had to wipe their tears to see.

"What about the terrible two's?"

Noreen shook her head with a found smile on her face. "Chloe didn't really have them. She had what parents call the 'why' stage. I swear that started the second she started to talk until earlier today."

"Not to sound stupid or anything, but what's the why stage?"

"It where the kids ask why for everything you tell them. I finally found a way around her asking that all the time."

"What was that?"

"I told her the truth about everything, I even went on to explain how things worked. She got bored with the answers and would only ask why if she actually wanted to know the answer."

"That was smart of you."

"I know. Now, you didn't answer my question. Do you want kids of your own?"

Spencer looked at her, then stared off into space for a long time. When Noreen didn't think he would answer her, he spoke, "I don't know. I don't want to push this back on you, and don't be offended by what I'm about to say, but are you ready to have a child again at your age? Not that you're old, but Chloe will be leaving for college in four or five years, or the military, I won't rule that out. Whatever she picks I'll support her. Are you willing to start all over at the age you are now. I know she said she wanted siblings, but what if we wanted to travel after she left for college? Would we be able to that with a small child in tow?"

"I never thought of it that way. I never planned on having a man in my life. As I told you before, the second I told Tyler I was pregnant, he disappeared.

The only reason I knew he heard what I said was because he had his lawyer send me all the paperwork where he relinquished all of his rights to her."

"What does that actually mean?"

"It means that he signed the papers saying that he didn't want any responsibility. The only downfall with that is two things that I could see."

"Which were?"

"One, I couldn't go after him for child support. However, with that paperwork they sent me a hefty check. I was going to rip it up and send the pieces back to them, but I'm not stupid. I put that money into an account and after Chloe was born, I put her name on it. I haven't touched a dime of it in all these years."

"Wow, so she might be set for college?"

"She doesn't know about it. I'll tell her when she's eighteen and has to make the decision of what she wants to do after she graduates. Like you said, I' will support her if she decides to further her education through college, or join the military."

"You know, I took on-line classes between my assignments. I have two master's degrees, all on Uncle Sam's dime."

"Oh, wow, I never thought of that being an option. I thought you had to be retired from the military for the GI bill to work."

"Nope, active military personnel can get their degree while still serving."

235

"That's something to think about."

"You said that letter from the sperm donor had two downfalls. What was the other one?"

"I don't think of it as actually a downfall, but because he sent the papers before she was even born, it stated that his name wasn't to be put on her birth certificate, and I had to give her my last name. Hell, when all this happened, I didn't even know what I was having. I was only thirteen weeks pregnant."

"How long is a pregnancy?"

"Forty weeks."

"Wow, so he cut bait and ran early."

"Yes, the only good thing, other than that sizable check I put in her account, is that if I ever decide to marry, my husband has a clear path to adopting her and giving her his last name."

"Really?" Spencer sat up in excitement. "So, if you and I ever got married, I could adopt her, and all three of us could have the last name of Barnes?"

"Yes."

"Damn, that's something to think about. As for your question about if I want to be a father or not? I'm not being difficult, but I can't answer that honestly right now. I never thought this topic would ever be discussed, like ever. I would need a little more time to tell you my answer."

"I respect that. Thank you for your honesty. I would have to think long and hard about whether I would want to have another child again. I'm thirty-four right now; it might be years before I can conceive. I don't want to be forty and pregnant. Not that there's anything wrong with that. It's just that the older I get, the more complications could develop during the pregnancy. I was young when I had Chloe and didn't have any problems, but I've heard that some women develop diabetes during pregnancy. The older you are, the more complications."

"I'll tell you right now. I wouldn't want you to go through that just to make me a father. Now that I know it's a viable option, I would be ecstatic to be able to adopt Chloe and call her my own." He studied her expression intently, watched her as she looked away, and wiped a tear from the corner of her eye. He hoped it was a happy tear. When she had herself under control, she looked at him with a sappy, albeit happy grin. She started laughing.

"What's so funny?"

"It's not exactly funny, it's just a request."

"Which is?"

"How about we put a pin in all this baby talk, with the promise to revisit this discussion at a later date."

"I can do that."

"Good, now, if you still have condoms, how about putting one of them to good use?" She looked at him with a gigantic grin, then giggled at his look. "If you have the energy for it, that is."

"That, I can do." Spencer said as he threw the covers back, stood up, and as naked as the day he was born, he strode over to where he'd placed his jeans earlier, and withdrew his wallet. He pulled out a condom, and strode toward the bed. For the next hour, he proved to her just how much energy he had when it came to loving her. It was to the point that she had to have him stop so she could catch her breath. Once she was better, he spent several more hours loving her, until they both fell into an exhausted heap, falling asleep with gigantic smiles on their faces.

EPILOGUE

"OBJECTION!" The district attorney jumped to his feet to shout out his reaction to the question the defense attorney had just asked Spencer. They were at the trial for Jennifer for her crimes. It turned out the DA's office charged her with two accounts of attempted murder, and one count of grand larceny. The first attempt had been when she'd thrown the knife where Spencer had stepped in front of it. The second attempt had been when she arrived at the door and pointed a gun at Spencer. Jennifer had thought she was going to scare Noreen into dropping the charges against her. What Jennifer hadn't realized, or if she had, she didn't acknowledge it, but Noreen had never pressed any charges against her. It had been Mattie and Spencer to file them formally with Sheriff Faulkner. Now they were sitting in a court room at her trial. Spencer just happened to be on the witness stand.

"Sustained," the judge said and glared at the defense attorney.

"Mr. Barnes, is it true that you were let go of your last job because of insubordination?"

"OBJECTION!" The DA, who hadn't sat back down yet, screamed at the judge.

"Sustained."

Spencer felt like he was watching a tennis match, and was tired of the questions being asked by the defense attorney. He never got her name, and frankly, he didn't care to know it. He settled back in the chair, and glanced out over the courtroom. He subtly covered his mouth when he saw Noreen, Chloe, and his buddies roll their eyes at him. Logan even twirled a finger next to his ear, indicating the defense lawyer was crazy. He only gave a subtle nod.

"Mr. Barnes," the defense attorney said, and Spencer had to cough to bring himself back to the matter at hand. He couldn't wait to get off the stand, he had better things to do than sit here and listen to the two lawyers argue back and forth.

"Mr. Barnes, what were the circumstances of the termination from your last employer?"

"OBJECTION! Your honor, I'd like to approach the bench."

"Sustained, and yes, both of you can approach."

Spencer watched as the two lawyers walked up to

the judge and he covered the microphone. He was close enough to be able to hear what they were saying.

"Your Honor, Ms. Davies is continuing to ask the witness questions she knows she's not supposed to ask. We discussed this in your chamber just yesterday. I'd like to make a motion to remove this witness from the list, or she come up with better questions."

"I agree." The judge nodded and turned a glare onto Ms. Davies. "You will stop asking this witness about his former employer. That is not pertinent to this case. If you can't do so, then I will dismiss this witness from your list. "Why are you repeatedly asking the wrong questions? Do you need to go back to law school?"

"No, Your Honor. I'm just trying to establish his creditability as a witness, that's all."

"I can answer that," Spencer leaned toward them as he butted into their conversation. "However, I can't answer the questions about my former employer."

"Why the hell not?" Ms. Davies demanded. Spencer saw how frustrated she was.

"Ever hear of a 'gag order'?" he asked snidely. That seemed to shut her up, and she shook her head.

"Fine."

"One more question regarding Mr. Barnes' former employer, and he's off the stand."

"Yes, Sir."

They went back to their stations, and Ms. Davies walked up to him. "Since I'm unable to ask the questions I want," she said as she looked at the jury. "I'm trying to understand the character of the witness." She turned to Spencer and then looked at the judge and DA before asking her next question.

"Mr. Barnes, what makes you the person you are today?" When no one said anything, Spencer looked at the two men and they both nodded to him. He settled in his chair to give his answer.

"As was discussed in the judge's chambers yesterday and earlier today, I am not allowed to give certain details about my former employer. However, I can tell you that I served twenty-three years in the military. For the last eighteen of those years, I was a Navy SEAL. I severed my country to the best of my ability. I went on missions that would cause the regular person to have nightmares, or end up in some sort of institution. I loved my job. If it wasn't for on particular person, I would still be serving my country today."

"Can you elaborate on that, Mr. Barnes?"

"I'll try, but again, I can't give you minute details, I can only give generalities."

"I understand, please tell us what you can."

"I was bullied out of my career by someone that ran the war behind a computer screen. While they were in the general area of the action, they never had boot on the ground. By that, I mean they were never shot at, never fired a weapon back at the shooter, never got blood on their hands. They ran their job though the computer. To the best of my knowledge, this person was pissed that our last mission was successful. By the time we arrived back home, there were some lies, doctored documents, and left out information waiting for us. Because of those, I was terminated. However," Spencer said sternly and held up his hand toward her. "I am under a gag order from the United States military not to say any more. I can say more about why I did what I did."

"You mean violating my clients privacy by filming her while she was at her job?"

"No, I mean by witnessing a crime, and getting it on videotape. Because of what happened to me at my last job, which is still an open and ongoing case, I learned the hard way not to take anyone's word for anything. I abhor bullies, and people that think they can bend the law. Even you, Ms. Davies thought you could get away with bending the law."

"How dare you, I was doing my job?"

"Were you? It sounded like you thought you could badger me with your questions that were the same one, just worded differently. That's badgering, and in my book, that's bullying. I saw a crime, I videotaped it. I was sitting at the table with the sheriff of this county and he didn't say anything to stop me. Let me ask you this, what's the difference if I videotaped it with my own personal cell phone, or if there had been cameras in the workplace? Nothing. I on the other hand, didn't blast what I saw all over social media, I talked to the sheriff, and he handled it to the best of his ability. I did nothing wrong except to help out a victim."

"Aren't you dating the victim? Did you take the video in question so you could get your girlfriend more money that my client earned?"

Spencer couldn't help it, he snorted a laugh. "Have you seen the video, Ms. Davies?"

"Answer the question," the judge said.

Spencer shook his head and looked directly at the lawyer as he answered coldly, he saw her shiver, and he knew he had gotten his point across. "Before the day in question, about the restaurant deal, I had never laid eyes on Noreen Rafferty before. We never started dating until three days later."

"Yet you shoved her behind you when my client allegedly threw a knife in her direction."

Spencer cocked his head to the side and stared at her like she'd gone stark raving mad. "Hello, I was a soldier for twenty-three years, plus I am a man. I've been trained in all situations, and it started at my mother's knees. Women are to be protected at all times. I shoved Ms. Rafferty behind me and stepped in the path of the knife. Otherwise, it would have hit her square in the face."

"And the incident with the toy gun? You were at Ms. Rafferty's home."

"Yes, we were dating, I was visiting. I opened the door and saw a gun pointed at me. I reacted. Again, my training kicked in. I didn't know it was a toy gun until after the police arrived. I defused the situation with the best of my ability."

"Do you feel you used excessive force?"

"No, I used my training the best of my ability. I disarmed Ms. Lockwood, and took her down. I then restrained her until the proper authorities arrived. Standing there was a gun pointed to my face and waiting for the police wasn't an option. I knew I had the situation under control. To the best of my knowledge, I didn't harm Ms. Lockwood. Please tell me if I did otherwise."

Ms. Davies didn't respond, she looked at her papers on the desk, shuffled them, then looked up at him. Spencer knew then and there, she knew she was losing her case. "The gun was a toy."

"It didn't look like that from where I was standing. How many cases are in this country where people pulled toy guns on cops and they were shot and killed for it? From the other end of that gun, it looks real. Me, as well as those police officers are trained to make a decision in less than two seconds. While we make that decision, we have at least a million things going through our minds."

"Like what?"

"Will I see my loved ones after this, will I lose my job, is that gun real or fake, did I update my will, will the bullet hurt, will I die, is this some type of gang initiation? Stuff like that." He saw the shock on Jennifer's face and stopped talking.

"No further questions," Ms. Davies said. "The defense rests."

"Mr. Barnes," the DA said as he stood, buttoned up his jacket, and approached the witness stand. "I'm going to play the two videos for the jury. The ones you took. I'd like to question you afterward."

"Whatever?" Spencer shrugged and looked at his watch. He sighed in relief when he saw he had plenty of time. He looked over at the judge and saw his smirk. For the next forty-five minutes, the videos were played, and questions were answered. Every single time the DA asked a question, Ms. Davies would object. Each time it was overruled and Spencer answered the questions.

"That's all I have for this witness," the DA said as he went back to his table and unbuttoned his jacket before he sat back down.

"Okay, I'd like to call a recess for lunch. Meet back here in two hours." The judge banged his gavel, and everyone rose. As the courtroom began to empty, Spencer looked at Noreen and Chloe with a smile.

"Now," he said to her.

"Okay," she grinned as she rose from her seat, grabbed her daughter's hand, a large purse and left the courtroom.

"You guys going to lunch?" Spencer asked the

guys he worked with, before they could answer he grinned at them. "I'd like for you to stick around for a few minutes." He studied them intently. "Which one of you would like to step up and be my best man?"

"Huh?" They all asked in shock.

"Noreen and I are getting married today. She just went to change into a dress. I had you guys here for the trial, not because I was testifying, but because I want you here for my wedding. Later, I can go back home and introduce Noreen and Chloe to my family. We can have a little get together there. But here, I didn't want to wait."

The men shook his hands, and their women hugged him and kissed his cheek. Ten minutes later, Noreen reappeared in an ivory knee-length dress with a subtle lace overlay. Chloe stood beside her in a pale blue dress.

"You ready?" Came a voice from the front of the room and they all turned to see the judge that had been at the bench standing there. Beside him was woman wearing a set of robes like he did. Spencer took Noreen's hand and they walked toward the front of the room.

"This is Judge Woolery. Because I'm the judge presiding over the case you just testified at, I didn't thing it would be appropriate for me to perform this ceremony today. I asked Judge Woolery to step in for me."

"Thank you," Spencer said and looked at Noreen. "You okay with this?"

"Yes," she breathed silently. "I don't care who presides over it, I just want to be your wife."

"And daughter!" Chloe chimed in.

They all took their positions, and fifteen minutes later, Spencer looked at Noreen, took her hands in his, held them tightly, and said loud and clear. "I Spencer Barnes do promise to love you to the best of my ability, in sickness and in health, for richer and for poorer. I promise to love you more and more each day. This is my promise to you." He barely heard what the judge said after that, not until he was told he could kiss his bride. When they broke apart, they smiled at one another.

"Here," the first judge said as he passed a folder between them. "I'll let you settle up the paperwork with Judge Woolery, but this is the paperwork you asked for earlier in the week."

Spencer took it with a grin, and shoved it beneath his arm as he finished up the paperwork. On the way out the door, Chloe asked what was in the folder.

"Not that I'm getting into your business or anything, but I'm curious."

Spencer stopped, and with his hand in Noreen's he turned to look at the young woman.

"It's not a secret, I was going to tell you when we got home. It's all the forms I need to fill out in order for me to adopt you."

"You'd be my father, for real?"

"Yes, and I promise you right here and now, that not matter what roadblocks my appear in this process or in your life, I will do the best of my ability to get you over them. As any father would do." He had to brace himself for the impact of her slamming into him. With their arms around each other, Chole cried into his neck.

"I love you, Dad."

"And I love you, Chloe." He kissed the top of her head, then stared down at Noreen. "And I love you, too." Their friends left the happy little family alone for a few minutes before they all gathered themselves and went out to lunch to celebrate their wedding.

THE END

THANK you for taking the time to read this. If you enjoyed this book, please give it some love and leave a review at your preferred site.

YOU CAN CONTACT ME AT:

E-mail: deannalrowley@yahoo.com

Facebook: https://www.facebook.com/Author-Deanna-L-Rowley-106623544172360

Website: https://deannarowley.com/

Goodreads: https://www.goodreads.com/search?q=Deanna+L.+Rowley&qid=1KYE0zxcp5

BookBub: https://www.bookbub.com/profile/deanna-l-rowley

AGAIN, thank you for taking the time to read this.

Please continue reading for other books available for sale and on pre-order.

TEAM RAPTOR

Darius' Promise - Jen Talty
Simon's Promise - Leanne Tyler
Nash's Promise - Stacey Wilk
Spencer's Promise - Deanna L. Rowley
Logan's Promise - Kris Norris

Thank you for reading Spencer's Promise. Please feel free to leave an honest review! I love to hear feedback from readers.

ABOUT DEANNA L. ROWLEY

Deanna has loved to read all her life. She was in the third grade when she fell in love with books while working in the school library. She turned that love of reading into writing. Now Deanna can be found in her writing cave, sharing her keyboard with her furbaby, reading, or making quilts.

BOOKS BY DEANNA L. ROWLEY

LOVE FOUND SERIES

Love Doesn't Exist

Love Is Fleeting

Love Conquers All

SPIES, LIES & RIDES

Aimee's Dilemma

Hank's Mission

Colt's Quest

George's Goal

Hogan's Handful

Witt's Warriors

John's Journey

Gary's Turn

STORMVILLE – SUSPENSEFUL SEDUCTION WORLD

Samantha A. Cole

Bourbon Blaze

Neil's Wish

Ginny's Slow Sizzle

CAPE Investigations Series

Claiming Mia

Fighting For Kora

Team Raptor

Spencer's Promise

Not Her Series:

Not Her Dom

Not Her Choice

Not Her Rebound

Not Her Problem #1

Not Her Problem #2

Not Her His Fault

Not Her Doing

Stand-alone:

Double Trouble for Kali

Ruby's Destiny

Molly's Return

Writing as RL Dean

Wade's World

BROTHERHOOD PROTECTORS
ORIGINAL SERIES BY ELLE JAMES

Brotherhood Protectors Yellowstone

Saving Kyla (#1)

Saving Chelsea (#2)

Saving Amanda (#3)

Saving Liliana (#4)

Saving Breely (#5)

Saving Savvie (#6)

Saving Jenna (#7)

Brotherhood Protectors Colorado

SEAL Salvation (#1)

Rocky Mountain Rescue (#2)

Ranger Redemption (#3)

Tactical Takeover (#4)

Colorado Conspiracy (#5)

Rocky Mountain Madness (#6)

Free Fall (#7)

Colorado Cold Case (#8)

Fool's Folly (#9)

Colorado Free Rein (#10)

Rocky Mountain Venom (#11)

ABOUT ELLE JAMES

ELLE JAMES also writing as MYLA JACKSON is a *New York Times* and *USA Today* Bestselling author of books including cowboys, intrigues and paranormal adventures that keep her readers on the edges of their seats. When she's not at her computer, she's traveling, snow skiing, boating, or riding her ATV, dreaming up new stories. Learn more about Elle James at www.ellejames.com

Website | Facebook | Twitter | GoodReads | Newsletter | BookBub | Amazon

Or visit her alter ego Myla Jackson at mylajackson.com
Website | Facebook | Twitter | Newsletter

Follow Me!
www.ellejames.com
ellejamesauthor@gmail.com

Printed in Great Britain
by Amazon